KT-494-686

For Penny Allen

Ian McEwan

The Comfort of Strangers

PICADOR
published by Pan Books

First published 1981 by Jonathan Cape Ltd
This Picador edition published 1982 by Pan Books Ltd,
Cavaye Place, London sw10 9pg
© Ian McEwan 1981
isbn 0 330 26829 5
Filmset by
Northumberland Press Ltd, Gateshead, Tyne and Wear
Printed and bound in Great Britain by
Richard Clay (The Chaucer Press) Ltd, Bungay, Suffolk

This book is sold subject to the condition that it
shall not, by way of trade or otherwise, be lent, re-sold,
hired out, or otherwise circulated without the publisher's prior
consent in any form of binding or cover other than that in which
it is published and without a similar condition including this
condition being imposed on the subsequent purchaser

how we dwelt in two worlds
the daughters and the mothers
in the kingdom of the sons

Adrienne Rich

Travelling is a brutality. It forces you to trust strangers and to lose sight of all that familiar comfort of home and friends. You are constantly off balance. Nothing is yours except the essential things – air, sleep, dreams, the sea, the sky – all things tending towards the eternal or what we imagine of it.

Cesare Pavese

chapter
one

Each afternoon, when the whole city beyond the dark green shutters of their hotel windows began to stir, Colin and Mary were woken by the methodical chipping of steel tools against the iron barges which moored by the hotel café pontoon. In the morning these rusting, pitted hulks, with no visible cargo or means of propulsion, would be gone; towards the end of each day they reappeared, and their crews set to inexplicably with their mallets and chisels. It was at this time, in the clouded, late afternoon heat, that customers began to gather on the pontoon to eat ice cream at the tin tables, and their voices too filled the darkened hotel room, rising and falling in waves of laughter and dissent, flooding the brief silences between each piercing blow of the hammers.

They woke, so it seemed to them, simultaneously, and lay still on their separate beds. For reasons they could no longer define clearly, Colin and Mary were not on speaking terms. Two flies gyrated lazily round the ceiling light, along the corridor a key turned in a lock and footsteps advanced and receded. At last, Colin rose, pushed the shutters ajar and went to the bathroom to shower. Still absorbed in the aftermath of her dreams, Mary turned on her side as he passed and stared at the wall. The steady trickle of water next door made a soothing sound, and she closed her eyes once more.

Each evening, in the ritual hour they spent on their balcony before setting out to find a restaurant, they had been listening patiently to the other's dreams in exchange for the luxury of recounting their own. Colin's dreams were those that psycho-analysts recommend, of flying, he said, of crumbling teeth, of appearing naked before a seated stranger. For Mary the hard mattress, the unaccustomed heat, the barely explored city were combining to set loose in her sleep a turmoil of noisy, argumentative dreams which, she complained, numbed her waking hours; and the fine old churches, the altar-pieces, the stone bridges over canals, fell dully on her retina, as on a distant screen. She dreamed most frequently of her children, that they were in danger, and that she was too incompetent or muddled to help them. Her own childhood became confused with theirs. Her son and daughter were her contemporaries, frightening her with their insistent questions. Why did you go away without us? When are you coming back? Will you meet us off the train? No, no, she tried to tell them, you are meant to be meeting *me*. She told Colin that she dreamed her children had climbed into bed with her, one on either side, and there they lay, bickering all night over her sleeping body. Yes I did. No you didn't. I told you. No you didn't . . . until she woke exhausted, her hands pressed tight against her ears. Or, she said, her ex-husband steered her into a corner and began to explain patiently, as he once had, how to operate his expensive Japanese camera, testing her on its intricacies at every stage. After many hours she started to sigh and moan, begging him to stop, but nothing could interrupt the relentless drone of explanation.

The bathroom window gave on to a courtyard and at this hour it too came alive with sounds from adjacent rooms and the hotel kitchens. The moment Colin turned his shower off, the man across the way under his shower began, as on the previous evenings, to sing his duet from *The Magic Flute*. His

voice rising above the torrential thunder of water and the
smack and squelch of well-soaped skin, the man sang
with the total abandon of one who believes himself to be
without an audience, cracking and yodelling the higher
notes, tra-la-ing the forgotten words, bellowing out the
orchestral parts. '*Mann und Weib, und Weib und Mann,
Together make a godly span.*' When the shower was turned
off, the singing subsided to a whistle.

Colin stood in front of the mirror, listening, and for no
particular reason began to shave for the second time that
day. Since their arrival, they had established a well-ordered
ritual of sleep, preceded on only one occasion by sex, and
now the calm, self-obsessed interlude during which they
carefully groomed themselves before their dinner-time stroll
through the city. In this time of preparation, they moved
slowly and rarely spoke. They used expensive, duty-free
colognes and powders on their bodies, they chose their
clothes meticulously and without consulting the other, as
though somewhere among the thousands they were soon to
join, there waited someone who cared deeply how they
appeared. While Mary did her yoga on the bedroom floor,
Colin would roll a marihuana joint which they would smoke
on their balcony and which would enhance that delightful
moment when they stepped out of the hotel lobby into the
creamy evening air.

While they were out, and not only in the mornings, a
maid came and tidied the beds, or removed the sheets, if she
thought that was necessary. Unused to hotel life, they were
inhibited by this intimacy with a stranger they rarely saw.
The maid took away used paper tissues, she lined up their
shoes in the cupboard in a tidy row, she folded their dirty
clothes into a neat pile on a chair and arranged loose change
into little stacks along the bedside table. Rapidly, however,
they came to depend on her and grew lazy with their
possessions. They became incapable of looking after one

another, incapable, in this heat, of plumping their own pillows, or of bending down to retrieve a dropped towel. At the same time they had become less tolerant of disorder. One late morning, they returned to their room to find it as they had left it, simply uninhabitable, and they had no choice but to go out again and wait until it had been dealt with.

The hours before their afternoon sleep were equally well-defined, though less predictable. It was midsummer, and the city overflowed with visitors. Colin and Mary set out each morning after breakfast with their money, sunglasses and maps, and joined the crowds who swarmed across the canal bridges and down every narrow street. They dutifully fulfilled the many tasks of tourism the ancient city imposed, visiting its major and minor churches, its museums and palaces, all treasure-packed. In the shopping streets they spent time in front of window displays, discussing presents they might buy. So far, they had yet to enter a shop. Despite the maps, they frequently became lost, and could spend an hour or so doubling back and round, consulting (Colin's trick) the position of the sun, to find themselves approaching a familiar landmark from an unexpected direction, and still lost. When the going was particularly hard, and the heat more than usually oppressive, they reminded each other, sardonically, that they were 'on holiday'. They passed many hours searching for 'ideal' restaurants, or relocating the restaurant of two days before. Frequently, the ideal restaurants were full or, if it was past nine o'clock in the evening, just closing; if they passed one that wasn't, they sometimes ate in it long before they were hungry.

Alone, perhaps, they each could have explored the city with pleasure, followed whims, dispensed with destinations and so enjoyed or ignored being lost. There was much to wonder at here, one needed only to be alert and to attend. But they knew one another much as they knew themselves, and their intimacy, rather like too many suitcases, was a matter of perpetual concern; together they moved slowly, clumsily, effecting lugubrious compromises, attending to delicate shifts of mood, repairing breaches. As individuals they did not easily take offence; but together they managed to offend each other in surprising, unexpected ways; then the offender – it had happened twice since their arrival – became irritated by the cloying susceptibilities of the other, and they would continue to explore the twisting alleyways and sudden squares in silence, and with each step the city would recede as they locked tighter into each other's presence.

Mary stood up from her yoga and, after carefully considering her underwear, began to dress. Through the half-open french window she could see Colin on the balcony. Dressed in all white, he sprawled in the aluminium and plastic beach-chair, his wrist dangling near the ground. He inhaled, tilted his head and held his breath, and breathed smoke across the pots of geraniums that lined the balcony wall. She loved him, though not at this particular moment. She put on a silk blouse and a white cotton skirt and, as she sat down on the edge of the bed to fasten her sandals, picked up a tourist guide from the bedside table. In other parts of the country, according to the photographs, were meadows, mountains, deserted beaches, a pather that wound through a forest to a lake. Here, in her only free month of the year, the commitment was to museums and restaurants. At the sound of Colin's chair creaking, she crossed to the dressing-table and began to brush her hair with short, vigorous strokes.

Colin had brought the joint indoors for Mary, and she had refused it – a quick murmur of 'No thanks' – without turning in her seat. He lingered behind her, staring into the mirror with her, trying to catch her eye. But she looked straight ahead at herself and continued to brush her hair. He traced the line of her shoulder with his finger. Sooner or later, the silence would have to break. Colin turned to leave, and changed his mind. He cleared his throat, and rested his hand firmly on her shoulder. Outside there was the beginning of a sunset to watch, and indoors there were negotiations which needed to be opened. His indecision was wholly drug-induced and was of the tail-chasing kind that argued that if he moved away now, having touched her, she might, conceivably at least, be offended ... but then, she was continuing to brush her hair, long after it was necessary, and it seemed she was waiting for Colin to leave ... and why? ... because she sensed his reluctance to stay and was already offended? ... but was he reluctant? Miserably, he ran his finger along the line of Mary's spine. She now held the handle of the brush in one hand and rested the bristles in the open palm of the other, and continued to stare ahead. Colin leaned forward and kissed her nape, and when she still did not acknowledge him, he crossed the room with a noisy sigh and returned to the balcony.

Colin settled in his chair. Above him was a vast dome of clear sky, and he sighed again, this time in contentment. The workmen on the barges had put away their tools and now stood in a group facing out towards the sunset, smoking cigarettes. On the hotel café pontoon, the clientele had moved on to aperitifs, and the conversations from the tables were muted and steady. Ice chimed in glasses, the heels of the efficient waiters ticked mechanically across the pontoon boards. Colin stood up and watched the passers-by in the street below. Tourists, many of them elderly, in their best summer suits and dresses, moved along the pavement in reptilian slow motion. Now and then a couple stopped to stare approvingly at the customers on the pontoon drinking against their gigantic backcloth of sunset and reddened water. One elderly gentleman positioned his wife in the foreground and half-knelt with thin, trembling thighs, to take a picture. The drinkers at a table immediately behind the woman raised their glasses good-naturedly towards the camera. But the photographer, intent on spontaneity, straightened and, with a sweeping gesture of his free hand, tried to usher them back on the path of their unselfconscious existence. It was only when the drinkers, all young men, lost interest, that the old man lifted the camera to his face and bent his unsteady legs again. But now his wife had moved a few feet to one side and was interested in something in her hand. She was turning her back to the camera in order to encourage the last rays of sun into her handbag. Her husband called to her sharply and she moved smartly back into position. The closing snap of the handbag clasp brought the young men to life. They arranged themselves in their seats, lifted their glasses once more and made broad, innocent smiles. With a little moan of irritation the old man pulled his wife away by the wrist, while the young men, who barely noticed them leave, re-routed their toasts and smiles towards each other.

Mary appeared at the french window, a cardigan draped around her shoulders. With excited disregard for the state of play between them, Colin immediately set about recounting the little drama in the street below. She stood at the balcony wall, watching the sunset while he spoke. She did not shift her gaze when he gestured towards the young men at their table, but she nodded faintly. Colin could not reproduce the vague misunderstandings that constituted, according to him, the main interest of the story. Instead, he heard himself exaggerate its small pathos into vaudeville, perhaps in an attempt to gain Mary's full attention. He described the elderly gentleman as 'incredibly old and feeble', his wife was 'batty beyond belief', the men at the table were 'bovine morons', and he made the husband give out 'an incredible roar of fury'. In fact the word 'incredible' suggested itself to him at every turn, perhaps because he feared that Mary did not believe him, or because he did not believe himself. When

17

he finished, Mary made a short 'mm' sound through a half smile.

They stood several feet apart and continued to stare across the water in silence. The large church across the broad channel which they had often talked of visiting was now a silhouette and, nearer, a man in a small boat returned his binoculars to their case and knelt to restart the outboard motor. Above them and to their left, the green neon hotel-sign came on with an abrupt, aggressive crackle which subsided into a low buzz. Mary reminded Colin that it was getting late, that they should be going soon before the restaurants closed. Colin agreed, but neither moved. Then Colin sat down in one of the beach-chairs, and not long after that Mary sat down too. Another short silence, and they reached for one another's hand. Little squeeze answered little squeeze. They moved their chairs closer and whispered apologies. Colin touched Mary's breasts, she turned and kissed first his lips and then, in a tender, motherly way, his nose. They whispered and kissed, stood up to embrace, and returned to the bedroom where they undressed in semi-darkness.

This was no longer a great passion. Its pleasures were in its unhurried friendliness, the familiarity of its rituals and procedures, the secure, precision-fit of limbs and bodies, comfortable, like a cast returned to its mould. They were generous and leisurely, making no great demands, and very little noise. Their lovemaking had no clear beginning or end and frequently concluded in, or was interrupted by, sleep. They would have denied indignantly that they were bored. They often said they found it difficult to remember that the other was a separate person. When they looked at each other they looked into a misted mirror. When they talked of the politics of sex, which they did sometimes, they did not talk of themselves. It was precisely this collusion that made them vulnerable and sensitive to each other, easily hurt by the rediscovery that their needs and interests were distinct. They conducted their arguments in silence, and reconciliations such as this were their moments of greatest intensity, for which they were deeply grateful.

They dozed, then dressed hurriedly. While Colin went to the bathroom, Mary returned to the balcony to wait. The hotel sign had been turned off. The street below was deserted, and on the pontoon two waiters were clearing away the cups and glasses. The few customers who remained were no longer drinking. Colin and Mary had never left the hotel so late, and Mary was to attribute much of what followed to this fact. She paced the balcony impatiently, inhaling the musty smell of geraniums. There were no restaurants open now, but on the far side of the city, if they could find it, was a late-night bar outside which a man sometimes stood with his hot-dog stand. When she was thirteen, still a conscientious, punctual schoolgirl alive with a hundred ideas for self-improvement, she had kept a notebook in which, every Sunday evening, she set out her goals for the week ahead. These were modest, achievable tasks, and it comforted her to tick them off as the week progressed: to practise the cello, to be kinder to her mother, to walk to school to save the bus fare. She longed for such comfort now, for time and events to be at least partially subject to control. She sleepwalked from moment to moment, and whole months slipped by without memory, without bearing the faintest imprint of her conscious will.

'Ready?' Colin called. She went inside, closing the french window behind her. She took the key from the bedside table, locked the door, and followed Colin down the unlit staircase.

chapter
two

Throughout the city, at the confluences of major streets, or
in the corners of the busiest square, were small, neatly
constructed kiosks or shacks which by day were draped with
newspapers and magazines in many languages, and with
tiers of postcards showing famous views, children, animals
and women who smiled when the card was tilted.

Inside the kiosk sat the vendor, barely visible through the
tiny hatch, and in virtual darkness. It was possible to buy
cigarettes here and not know whether it was a man or a
woman who sold them. The customer saw only the native
deep brown eyes, a pale hand, and heard muttered thanks.
The kiosks were centres of neighbourhood intrigue and
gossip; messages and parcels were left here. But tourists
asking for directions were answered with a diffident gesture
towards the display of maps, easily missed between the ranks
of lurid magazine covers.

A variety of maps was on sale. The least significant were
produced by commercial interests and, besides showing the
more obvious tourist attractions, they gave great prominence
to certain shops or restaurants. These maps were marked
with the principal streets only. Another map was in the form
of a badly printed booklet and it was easy, Mary and Colin
had found, to get lost as they walked from one page to
another. Yet another was the expensive, officially sanctioned
map which showed the whole city and named even the

narrowest of passageways. Unfolded, it measured four feet by three and, printed on the flimsiest of papers, was impossible to manage outdoors without a suitable table and special clips. Finally there was a series of maps, noticeable by their blue-and-white striped covers, which divided the city into five manageable sections, none of them, unfortunately, overlapping. The hotel was in the top quarter of map two, an expensive, inefficient restaurant at the foot of map three. The bar towards which they were now walking was in the centre of map four, and it was only when they passed a kiosk, shuttered and battened for the night, that Colin remembered that they should have brought the maps. Without them they were certain to get lost.

However, he said nothing. Mary was several feet ahead, walking slowly and evenly as though measuring out a distance. Her arms were folded and her head was lowered, defiantly contemplative. The narrow passageway had brought them on to a large, flatly lit square, a plain of cobbles, in the centre of which stood a war memorial of massive, rough-hewn granite blocks assembled to form a gigantic cube, topped by a soldier casting away his rifle. This was familiar, this was the starting point for nearly all their expeditions. But for a man stacking chairs outside a café, watched by a dog and, further off, another man, the square was deserted.

They crossed diagonally and entered a wider street of shops selling televisions, dishwashers and furniture. Each store prominently displayed its burglar-alarm system. It was the total absence of traffic in the city that allowed visitors the freedom to become so easily lost. They crossed streets without looking and, on impulse, plunged down narrower ones because they curved tantalizingly into darkness, or because they were drawn by the smell of frying fish. There were no signs. Without a specific destination, the visitors chose routes as they might choose a colour, and even the precise manner in which they became lost expressed their cumulative choices, their will. And when there were two together making choices? Colin stared at Mary's back. The street lighting had bleached her blouse of colour, and against the old blackened walls she shimmered, silver and sepia, like an apparition. Her fine shoulder-blades, rising and falling with her slow stride, made a rippling fan of creases across her silk blouse, and her hair, which was partly gathered at the back of her head with a butterfly clasp, swung backwards and forwards across her shoulders and nape.

She stopped at the window of a department store to examine an enormous bed. Colin drew level with her, lingered a moment, and then walked on. Two dummies, one dressed in pyjamas of pale blue silk, the other in a thigh-length nightie trimmed with pink lace, lay among the artfully dishevelled sheets. The display was not quite complete. The dummies were from the same mould, both bald, both smiling wondrously. They lay on their backs, but from the arrangement of their limbs – each lifted a hand painfully to its jaw – it was clear they were intended to be reclining on their side, facing each other fondly. It was the headboard, however, that had caused Mary to stop. Upholstered in black plastic, it spanned the width of the bed with a foot to spare on either side. It was designed, on the pyjama side at least, to resemble the control panel of a power station, or perhaps a light aircraft. Embedded in the shiny upholstery were a telephone, a digital clock, light-switches and dimmers, a cassette recorder and radio, a small refrigerated drinks cabinet and, towards the centre, like eyes rounded in disbelief, two voltmeters. The nightie side, dominated by an oval, rose-tinted mirror, was sparse by comparison. There was an inset make-up cabinet, a magazine rack and a nursery intercom. Balanced on top of the refrigerator was a cheque on which was written next month's date, the name of the department store, a huge sum and a signature in bold strokes. Mary noticed that the dummy in pyjamas was holding a pen. She took a couple of paces to one side and an imperfection in the plate glass caused the figures to stir. Then they were still, their arms and legs raised uselessly, like insects surprised by poison. She turned her back on the tableau. Colin was fifty yards along, on the other side of the street. Shoulders haunched, hands deep in his pockets, he was watching a book of carpet samples methodically turning its pages. She caught him up and they walked on in silence till they came to a fork at the end of the street and stopped.

Colin spoke in commiseration. 'You know, I was looking at that bed the other day too.'

Where the street divided there stood what must have once been an imposing residence, a palace. A row of stone lions stared down from beneath the rusting balcony on the first floor. The high-arched windows, flanked by finely grooved, pitted pillars, were blocked with corrugated tin which had been fly-posted, even on the second floor. Most of the announcements and pronouncements were from feminists and the far Left, and a few were from local groups opposed to the redevelopment of the building. High up, above the second floor, was a wooden board which announced in bright red lettering the name of the chain store that had acquired the site, and then in English, in quotation marks: 'The shop that puts *you* first!' Ranged outside the grand front door, like a line of premature customers, were plastic rubbish sacks. Hands on hips, Colin peered down one street, then crossed to peer down the other. 'We should have brought those maps.'

Mary had climbed the first steps of the palace and was reading the posters. 'The women are more radical here,' she said over her shoulder, 'and better organized.'

Colin had stepped back to compare the two streets. They ran straight for a considerable distance and eventually curved away from each other. 'They've got more to fight for,' he said. 'We came by this way before, but can you remember which way we went?' Mary was translating with difficulty a lengthy proclamation. 'Which way?' Colin said slightly louder.

Frowning, Mary ran her forefinger along the lines of bold print, and when she finished she exclaimed in triumph. She turned and smiled at Colin. 'They want convicted rapists castrated!'

He had moved to get a better view of the street to the right. 'And hands chopped off for theft? Look, I'm sure we passed that drinking fountain before, on the way to this bar.'

Mary turned back to the poster. 'No. It's a tactic. It's a way of making people take rape more seriously as a crime.'

Colin moved again and stood, with his feet firmly apart, facing the street on their left. It too had a drinking fountain. 'It's a way,' he said irritably, 'of making people take feminists less seriously.'

Mary folded her arms, and after a moment's pause set off slowly down the right-hand fork. She had regained her slow, precise pace. 'People take hanging seriously enough,' she said. 'A life for a life.'

Uneasily Colin watched her go. 'Wait a minute, Mary,' he called after her. 'Are you sure that's right?' She nodded without turning round. In the far distance, picked out momentarily by a streetlight, a figure was walking towards them. Somehow reassured by this, Colin caught up with her.

This too was a prosperous street, but its shops were huddled and exclusive, dedicated it seemed, to the sale of single items – in one shop a gold-framed landscape in cracked, muddied oils, in another a hand-made shoe, further on, a single camera lens mounted on a velvet plinth. The drinking fountain, unlike most in the city, actually worked. The dark stone of the surrounding step and the rim of its great bowl had been worn down and polished by centuries of use. Mary arranged her head under the tarnished brass faucet and drank. 'The water here,' she said between mouthfuls, 'tastes of fish.' Colin was staring ahead, waiting to see the approaching figure reappear beneath another lamp post. But there was nothing, except perhaps a rapid movement by a distant doorway, and that may have been a cat.

They had eaten their last meal, a shared plate of fried whitebait, twelve hours previously. Colin reached for Mary's hand. 'Can you remember if he sells anything apart from hot dogs?'

'Chocolate? Nuts?'

Their pace quickened and their footsteps resounded noisily on the cobbles, making the sound of only one pair of shoes. 'One of the eating capitals of the world,' Colin said, 'and we're walking two miles for hot dogs.'

'We're on holiday,' Mary reminded him. 'Don't forget that.'

He clapped his free hand to his forehead. 'Of course. I get too easily lost in details, like hunger and thirst. We are on holiday.'

They dropped hands, and as they walked on Colin hummed to himself. The street was narrowing and the shops had given way on both sides to high, dark walls, broken at irregular intervals by deeply recessed doorways, and windows, small and square, set high up and criss-crossed with iron bars.

'This is the glass factory,' Mary said with satisfaction. 'We tried to come here on our first day.' They slowed down, but did not stop.

Colin said, 'We must have been round the other side then, because I've never been here before.'

'We queued outside one of these doors while we were waiting.'

Colin wheeled round on her, incredulous, exasperated.

'That wasn't our first day,' he said loudly. 'Now you're completely confused. It was seeing the queue that made us decide to go to the beach, and we didn't go there till the third day.' Colin had stopped to say this, but Mary kept on walking. He caught up with her in skipping steps.

'It might have been the third day,' she was saying as though to herself, 'but this is where we were.' She pointed at a doorway several yards ahead and, as if summoned, a squat figure stepped out of the dark into a pool of streetlight and stood blocking their path.

'Now look what you've done,' Colin joked, and Mary laughed.

The man laughed too and extended his hand. 'Are you tourists?' he asked in self-consciously precise English and, beaming, answered himself. 'Yes, of course you are.'

Mary stopped directly in front of him and said, 'We're looking for a place where we can get something to eat.'

Colin meanwhile was sidling past the man. 'We don't have to explain ourselves, you know,' he said to Mary quickly. Even as he was speaking the man caught him cordially by the wrist and stretched out his other hand to take Mary's. She folded her arms and smiled.

'It is terribly late,' said the man. 'There is nothing in that direction, but I can show you a place this way, a very good place.' He grinned, and nodded in the direction they had come from.

He was shorter than Colin, but his arms were exceptionally long and muscular. His hands too were large, the backs covered with matted hair. He wore a tight-fitting black shirt, of an artificial, semi-transparent material, unbuttoned in a neat V almost to his waist. On a chain round his neck hung a gold imitation razor-blade which lay slightly askew on the thick pelt of chest hair. Over his shoulder he carried a camera. A cloying sweet scent of aftershave filled the narrow street.

'Look,' Colin said, trying to detach his wrist without appearing violent, 'we know there is a place down here.' The grip was loose but unremitting, a mere finger and thumb looped round Colin's wrist.

The man filled his lungs with air and appeared to grow an inch or two. 'Everything is closed,' he announced. 'Even the hot-dog stand.' He addressed himself to Mary with a wink. 'My name is Robert.' Mary shook his hand and Robert began to pull them back down the street. 'Please,' he insisted. 'I know just the place.'

After much effort over several paces, Colin and Mary brought Robert to a standstill and they stood in a close huddle, breathing noisily.

Mary spoke as though to a child. 'Robert, let go of my hand.' He released her immediately and made a little bow.

Colin said, 'And you'd better let go of me too.'

But Robert was explaining apologetically to Mary, 'I'd like to help you. I can take you to a very good place.' They set off again.

'We don't need to be *dragged* towards good food,' Mary said, and Robert nodded. He touched his forehead. 'I am, I am . . .'

'Wait a minute,' Colin interrupted.

'. . . always eager to practise my English. Perhaps too eager. I once spoke it perfectly. This way, please.' Mary was already walking on. Robert and Colin followed.

'Mary,' Colin called.

'English', Robert said, 'is a beautiful language, full of misunderstandings.'

Mary smiled over her shoulder. They had arrived once more at the great residence at the fork in the road. Colin pulled Robert to a halt and jerked his hand free. 'I'm sorry,' Robert said. Mary too had stopped and was examining the posters again. Robert followed her gaze to a crude stencil in red paint which showed a clenched fist enclosed within the sign used by ornithologists to denote the female of the species. Again he was apologetic, and seemed to assume personal responsibility for everything they could read. 'These are women who cannot find a man. They want to destroy everything that is good between men and women.' He added matter-of-factly, 'They are too ugly.' Mary watched him as she might a face on television.

'There,' Colin said, 'meet the opposition.'

She smiled sweetly at them both. 'Let's go and find this good food,' she said, just as Robert was indicating another poster and preparing to say more.

They took the left-hand fork and walked for ten minutes during which Robert's boisterous attempts to begin a conversation were met in silence, on Mary's part self-absorbed – she walked with her arms crossed again – and on Colin's faintly hostile – he kept his distance from Robert. They turned down an alley which descended by a series of worn steps to a diminutive square, barely thirty feet across, into which ran half a dozen smaller passageways 'Down there,' Robert said, 'is where I live. But it is too late for you to come there. My wife will be in bed.'

They made more turns to left and right, passing between tottering houses five storeys high, and shuttered grocers' shops with vegetables and fruit in wooden crates piled outside. An aproned shopkeeper appeared with a trolley-load of cases and called out to Robert who laughed and shook his head and raised his hand. When they reached a brightly lit doorway, Robert parted the yellowing strips of a plastic walk-through for Mary. He kept his hand on Colin's shoulder as they descended a steep flight of stairs into a cramped and crowded bar.

A number of young men, dressed similarly to Robert, sat on high stools at the bar, and several more were arranged in identical postures – all their weight on one foot – around a bulging juke-box of sumptuous curves and chromium scrolls.

A deep and pervasive blue emanated from the back of the machine and gave the faces of the second group a nauseous look. Everyone appeared to be smoking, or putting out his cigarette with swift, decisive jabs, or craning his neck forwards and pouting to have the cigarette lit. Since they all wore tight clothes, they had to hold their cigarette in one hand, the lighter and pack in the other. The song they were all listening to, for no one was talking, was loud and chirpily sentimental, with full orchestral accompaniment, and the man who sang it had a special sob in his voice for the frequent chorus which featured a sardonic 'ha ha ha', and it was here that several of the young men lifted their cigarettes and, avoiding each other's eyes, joined in with a frown and a sob of their own.

'Thank God I'm not a man,' Mary said, and tried to take Colin's hand. Robert had shown them to a table and had gone to the bar. Colin put his hands in his pockets, tipped back his chair and stared at the juke-box. 'Oh come on,' Mary said, prodding his arm. 'It was only a joke.'

The song ended in a triumphant symphonic climax and immediately began again. Behind the bar, glass shattered on the floor and there was a brief spate of slow hand-clapping.

Robert returned at last with a large, unlabelled bottle of red wine, three glasses and two well-fingered breadsticks, one of which was broken short. 'Today', he announced proudly above the din, 'the cook is ill.' With a wink at Colin he sat down and filled the glasses.

Robert began to ask them questions and at first they answered reluctantly. They told him their names, that they were not married, that they did not live together, at least, not now. Mary gave the ages and sexes of her children. They both stated their professions. Then, despite the absence of food, and helped on by the wine, they began to experience the pleasure, unique to tourists, of finding themselves in a place without tourists, of making a discovery, finding

29

somewhere real. They relaxed, they settled into the noise and smoke; they in turn asked the serious, intent questions of tourists gratified to be talking at last to an authentic citizen. In less than twenty minutes they had emptied the bottle. Robert told them that he had business interests, that he had grown up in London, that his wife was Canadian. When Mary asked how he met his wife, Robert said it was impossible to explain that without first describing his sisters and his mother, and these in turn could be explained only in terms of his father. It was clear he was preparing the way to telling them his story. 'Ha ha ha' was winding up to another crescendo, and at a table near the juke-box a man with curly hair sank his face in his hands. Robert shouted across the bar for another bottle of wine. Colin snapped the breadsticks in halves and shared them with Mary.

chapter three

The song ended, and all around the bar conversations were beginning, softly at first, a pleasant hum and susurration of the vowels and consonants of a foreign language; simple observations evoked in response single words or noises of assent; then pauses, random and contrapuntal, followed by more complex observations at a greater volume and in turn more elaborate replies. Within less than a minute, several apparently intense discussions were under way, as though various controversial subjects had been allotted and suitable adversaries grouped. If the juke-box were to have been played now, no one would have heard it.

Robert, staring at the glass which he held down on the table with both hands, seemed to be holding his breath and this caused Colin and Mary, who watched him closely, to breathe with difficulty. He appeared older than he had in the street. The oblique electric light picked out a set of almost geometrical lines like a grid across his face. Two lines, running from the base of each nostril to the corners of his mouth, formed a near-perfect triangle. Across his forehead were parallel furrows, and an inch below them, set at a precise right angle, was a single line at the bridge of his nose, a deep fold of flesh. He nodded to himself slowly and his massive shoulders drooped as he exhaled. Mary and Colin leaned forwards to catch the opening words of his story.

'All his life my father was a diplomat, and for many, many

years we lived in London, in Knightsbridge. But I was a lazy boy' – Robert smiled – 'and still my English is not perfect.' He paused, as though waiting to be contradicted. 'My father was a big man. I was his youngest child and only son. When he sat down he sat like this' – Robert adopted his previous tense and upright position and rested his hands squarely on his knees. 'All his life my father wore a moustache like this' – with forefinger and thumb Robert measured out an inch width beneath his nose – 'and when it turned to grey he used a little brush to make it black, such as ladies use for their eyes. Mascara.

'Everybody was afraid of him. My mother, my four sisters, even the ambassador was afraid of my father. When he frowned nobody could speak. At the dining-table you could not speak unless spoken to first by my father.' Robert began to raise his voice above the din around them. 'Every evening when there was to be a reception and my mother had to be dressed, we had to sit quietly with our backs straight and listen to my father reading aloud.

'Every morning he got out of bed at six o'clock and went to the bathroom to shave. No one was allowed out of bed until he had finished. When I was a little boy I was always next out of bed, quickly, and I went to the bathroom to smell him. Excuse me, he made a terrible smell, but it was covered with the smell of the shaving soap and his perfume. Even now, for me eau-de-Cologne is the smell of my father.

'I was his favourite, I was his passion. I remember – perhaps it happened many times – my older sisters, Eva and Maria, were fourteen and fifteen. It was dinner and they were pleading with him. Please, Papa. Please! And to everything he said No! They could not go on the school visit because there were going to be boys. They were not permitted to stop wearing white socks. They could not go to the theatre in the afternoon unless Mama went also. They could not have their friend to stay because she was a bad influence and never went to church. Then suddenly my father was standing behind my chair where I sat next to my mother, and laughing very loud. He took my napkin from my lap and tucked it into the front of my shirt. "Look!" he said. "Here is the next head of the family. You must remember to keep on the good side of Robert!" Then he made me settle the arguments, and all the time his hand was resting on me here, squeezing my neck between his fingers. My father would say, "Robert, may the girls wear silk stockings like their Mama?" And I, ten years old, would say very loudly, "No Papa". "May they go to the theatre without their Mama?" "Absolutely not, Papa." "Robert, may they have their friend to stay?" "Never, Papa!"

'I answered proudly, without knowing I was being used. Perhaps this was only once. To me it could have been every evening of my childhood. Then my father would walk back to his chair at the head of the table and pretend to be very sad. "I am sorry Eva, Maria, I was just beginning to change my mind, but now Robert says these things may not happen." And he laughed, and I would laugh too, I believed everything, every word. I would laugh until my mother put her hand on my shoulder and said, "Shush now, Robert".

'So! Did my sisters hate me? This time I know happened only once. It was the weekend and the house was empty for the whole afternoon. I went into our parents' bedroom with the same two sisters, Eva and Maria. I sat on the bed, and they went to my mother's dressing-table and took out all her things. First they painted their fingernails and waved them in the air to dry. They put creams and powders on their faces, they used lipstick, they pulled hairs from their eyebrows and brushed mascara on their lashes. They told me to shut my eyes while they took off their white socks and put on stockings from my mother's drawer. Then they stood, two very beautiful women, and looked at each other. And for an hour they walked about the house, looking over their shoulders into mirrors or window-panes, turning round and round in the centre of the drawing-room, or sitting very carefully on the edge of the armchair arranging their hair. Everywhere they went I followed, looking at them all the time, just looking. "Are we not beautiful, Robert?" they would say. They knew I was shocked because these were not my sisters, these were American film stars. They were delighted with themselves. They laughed and kissed each other for now they were real women.

'Later in the afternoon they went to the bathroom and washed everything off. In the bathroom they put away all the pots and jars and opened the windows so Mama would not smell her own perfumes. They folded the silk stockings and suspender belts away, exactly the way they had seen her do it. They closed the windows and we went downstairs to wait for our mother to come home, and all the time I was very excited. Suddenly the beautiful women had become my sisters again, tall schoolgirls.

'Then came dinner, and I was still excited. My sisters behaved as if nothing had happened. I was aware that my father was staring at me. I glanced up and he looked straight through my eyes, deep into my mind. Very slowly he put down his knife and fork, chewed and swallowed everything in his mouth and said, "Tell me, Robert, what have you been doing this afternoon?" I believed he knew everything, like God. He was testing me to find out if I was worthy enough to tell the truth. So, there was no point in lying. I told him everything, the lipstick, the powders, the creams and the perfumes, the stockings from my mother's drawer, and I told him, as if this would excuse everything, how carefully these things had been put away. I even mentioned the window. At first my sisters laughed and denied what I was saying. But as I went on and on, they became silent. When I had finished my father simply said, "Thank you, Robert," and went on eating. No one spoke for the rest of the meal. I dared not look in the direction of my sisters.

'After dinner and just before my bedtime I was called to
my father's study. This was a place where no one was
allowed, here were all the secrets of State. It was the biggest
room in the house, for sometimes my father received other
diplomats here. The windows and the deep red velvet
curtains went right up to the ceiling, and the ceiling had
gold leaf and great circular patterns. There was a
chandelier. Everywhere there were books in glass cases, and
the floor was very thick with rugs from all over the world,
and some were even hanging on the walls. My father was a
collector of rugs.

'He was sitting behind his enormous desk which was
covered with papers, and my two sisters were standing in
front of him. He made me sit on the other side of the room in
a great leather armchair that had once belonged to my
grandfather who also was a diplomat. No one spoke. It was
like a silent film. My father took a leather belt from a drawer
and beat my sisters – three very hard strokes each on the
backside – and Eva and Maria did not make a sound.
Suddenly I was outside the study. The door was closed. My
sisters had gone to their rooms to cry, I went up the stairs to
my own bedroom, and that was the end. My father never
mentioned this matter again.

'My sisters! They hated me. They had to have their
revenge. I think they talked of nothing else for weeks. This
also happened when the house was empty, no parents, no
cook, a month after my sisters were beaten, perhaps even
longer. First I must tell you that although I was the
favourite, there were many things I was not permitted.
Especially no sweet things to eat or drink, no chocolate, no
lemonade. My grandfather never allowed my father sweet
things, except fruit. It was bad for the stomach. But most
important, sweet things, especially chocolate, were bad for
boys. It made them weak in character, like girls. Perhaps

there was truth in this, only science can tell. Also, my father was concerned for my teeth, he wanted me to have teeth like his own, perfect. Outside I ate the sweets of other boys, but at home there was nothing.

'So, on this day Alice, the youngest sister, came to me in the garden and said, "Robert, Robert, come to the kitchen quickly. There is a treat for you. Eva and Maria have got a treat for you!" At first I did not go because I thought it might be a trick. But Alice said over and over again, "Come quickly Robert", so in the end I went and there in the kitchen were Eva and Maria, and Lisa, my other sister. And there on the table were two big bottles of lemonade, a cream cake, two packets of cooking chocolate and a big box of marshmallows. Maria said, "This is all for you", and immediately I was suspicious and said, "Why?" Eva said, "We want you to be kinder to us in future. When you have eaten all this you will remember how nice we are to you." This seemed reasonable, and the food looked so delicious, so I sat down and reached for the lemonade. But Maria put her hand on mine. "First," she said, "you must drink some medicine." "Why?" "Because you know how sweet things are bad for your stomach. If you are ill, Papa will know what you have been doing, and we will all be in trouble. This medicine will make everything all right." So I opened my mouth and Maria put in four big spoonfuls of some kind of oil. It tasted disgusting, but it did not matter because immediately I began to eat the cooking chocolate and the cream cake and to drink the lemonade.

'My sisters stood round the table and watched me. "Is it good?" they said, but I was eating so quickly I could hardly speak. I thought perhaps they were being so good to me because they knew that one day I would inherit my grandfather's house. After I had finished the first bottle of lemonade, Eva picked up the second and said, "I don't think he can drink this one as well. I'll put it away." And Maria said, "Yes, put it away. Only a *man* could drink two bottles of lemonade." I snatched the bottle from her and said, "Of course I can drink it," and all the girls said together, "Robert! That's impossible!" So of course I finished it, and the two bars of cooking chocolate, the marshmallows and all the cream cake, and my four sisters clapped their hands in rhythm. "Bravo Robert!"

'I tried to stand. The kitchen began to spin round me, and I badly needed to go to the lavatory. But suddenly Eva and Maria knocked me to the floor and held me down. I was too weak to fight, and they were much bigger. They had ready a long piece of rope and they tied my hands together behind my back. All the time Alice and Lisa were jumping up and down and singing, "Bravo Robert!" Then Eva and Maria dragged me to my feet and pushed me out of the kitchen, along the corridor, across the big hallway and into my father's study. They took the key from the inside, slammed the door and locked it. "Bye-bye Robert," they called through the keyhole. "Now you are big Papa in his study."

'I stood in the middle of this enormous room, beneath the chandelier, and at first I did not realize why I was there, and then I understood. I struggled with the knots, but they were too tight. I shouted and kicked at the door and banged it with my head, but the house was silent. I ran from one end of the room to the other looking for somewhere, and in every corner there were expensive rugs. Finally I could not help myself. The lemonade came, and not long after the cooking chocolate and cake, like a liquid. I was wearing short trousers, like an English schoolboy. And instead of standing still, and ruining only one rug, I ran everywhere, screaming and crying, as if my father was already chasing me.

'The key turned in the lock, the door flew open and in ran Eva and Maria. "Pooh!" they shouted. "Quick, quick! Papa is coming." They untied the rope, put the key back on the inside of the door and ran away, laughing like mad women. I heard my father's car stop in the driveway.

'At first I couldn't move. Then, I put my hand in my pocket and brought out a handkerchief and I went to the wall – yes, it was even on the walls, even on his desk – and I dabbed like so at an old Persian rug. Then I noticed my legs, they were almost black. The handkerchief was no use, it was too small. I ran to the desk and took some paper, and this was how my father found me, cleaning my knees with the affairs of State, and behind me the floor of his study was like a farmyard. I took two steps towards him, dropped to my knees and I was sick almost over his shoes, sick for a very long time. When I finished he had still not moved from the doorway. He still held his attaché case, and his face showed nothing. He looked down at where I had been sick and said, "Robert, have you been eating chocolate!" And I said, "Yes Papa but . . ." And that was enough for him. Later my mother came to see me in my bedroom, and in the morning a psychiatrist came and said there had been a trauma. But for my father it was enough that I had eaten chocolate. He beat me every night for three days and for many months he did not speak kindly to me. For many, many years I was not permitted in the study, not until I entered with my future wife. And to this day I never eat chocolate, and I have never forgiven my sisters.

'During the time I was being punished, my mother was the only one who talked to me. She made sure my father did not beat me too hard, and for only three nights. She was tall and very beautiful. Most often she wore white; white blouses, white scarves and white silk dresses to the diplomatic receptions. I remember her best in white. She spoke English very slowly, but everyone complimented her on its elegance, its perfection.

'As a boy, I had frequent bad dreams, very bad dreams. I also walked in my sleep, and sometimes I still do. Often my dreams made me wake in the middle of the night, and immediately I would call for her – "Mum", like an English boy. It was as if she was lying awake waiting, for straight away, far down the corridor where my parents' bedroom was, I heard the creak of the bed, the light switch, the little crack of a bone in her bare feet. And always, when she came to my room and said, "What is it, Robert?" I would say, "I want a glass of water". I never said, "I had a bad dream", or "I am frightened". Always, a glass of water which she brought from the bathroom and watched me drink. Then she kissed me on the head here, and immediately I was asleep. Sometimes this happened every night for many months, but she never left the water by my bed. She knew I had to have an excuse to call out to her in the middle of the night. But there was no need to explain. We were very close. Even after I was married, before she died, I used to take her my shirts every week.

'Whenever my father was away I slept in her bed, until I was ten years old. Then that came to a sudden end. One afternoon the wife of the Canadian ambassador was invited to tea. All day long there were preparations. My mother made sure my sisters and I knew how to hold a teacup and saucer. I was the one who was to go round the room with the plate of cakes and little sandwiches with no crusts. I was sent to the barber, and I was made to wear a red bow-tie, which I hated more than all the other things. The ambassador's wife had blue hair, something I had never seen before, and she brought with her a daughter, Caroline, who was twelve years old. Later I discovered that my father had said our families must become friendly for reasons of diplomacy and business. We sat very quietly and listened to the two mothers, and when the Canadian lady asked us a question,

39

we sat up straight and answered politely. Today children are not taught these things. Then my mother took the ambassador's wife away to show her the house and garden, and the children were left alone. My four sisters were wearing their party dresses and they all sat together on the big settee, so close they appeared as one person, one tangle of ribbon and lace and curls. When they were all together my sisters were frightening. Caroline sat on one wooden chair, and I sat on another. For several minutes no one spoke.

'Caroline had blue eyes and a small face, small like a monkey's. She had freckles across her nose, and on this afternoon she wore her hair in one long pigtail down her back. No one spoke, but from the corner of my eye I could see someone nudging someone else. Above our heads we could hear the sound of our mother and Caroline's mother as they moved from one room to another. Suddenly Eva said, "Miss Caroline, do you sleep with your mother?" And Caroline said, "No, do you?" Then Eva: "No, but Robert does."

'I went deep, deep red, and was ready to run from the room, but Caroline turned to smile at me and said, "I think that is really awfully sweet", and from that time on I was in love with her, and I no longer slept in my mother's bed. Six years later I met Caroline again, and two years after that we were married.'

Around them the bar was beginning to empty. The overhead lights had come on, and a bar-hand was sweeping the floor. Colin had dozed off for the last part of the story and slumped forwards, his head pillowed on his forearm. Robert picked up the empty wine bottles from their table and took them to the bar where he appeared to issue instructions. A second bar-hand came by to empty the ashtray into a bucket and wipe the table down.

When Robert returned Mary said, 'You didn't tell us much about your wife.'

He put into her hand a box of matches on which was printed the name and address of the bar. 'I'm here almost every night.' He closed her fingers around the box and squeezed. As he passed by Colin's chair, Robert reached out and ruffled his hair. Mary watched him go, sat yawning for a minute or two, then roused Colin and pointed him towards the stairs. They were the last to leave.

chapter
four

In one direction the street vanished into total darkness; in
the other, a diffused blue-grey light was making visible a
series of low buildings which descended like blocks cut in
granite and converged in the gloom where the street curved
away. Thousands of feet above, an attenuated finger of
cloud pointed across the line of the curve, and reddened.
A cool, salty wind blew along the street and stirred a
cellophane wrapper against the step on which Colin and
Mary were sitting. From behind a tightly shuttered window
immediately above their heads came a muffled snore and the
rasp of bedsprings. Mary leaned her head against Colin's
shoulder, and he leaned his against the wall behind him, in
the space between two drainpipes. A dog walked towards
them quickly from the lighter end of the street, its toenails
clicking primly on the worn stone. It did not pause as it
reached them, nor did it glance in their direction, and after
it had dissolved into the darkness, its complicated step could
still be heard.

'We should have brought the maps,' Colin said.

Mary leaned in closer against him. 'It hardly matters,' she
murmured. 'We're on holiday.'

They were woken an hour later by voices and laughter.
Somewhere a high-pitched bell chimed steadily. The light
was now flat, and the breeze was warm and moist, like
animal breath. Small children dressed in bright blue smocks

with black collars and cuffs surged past them, each bearing high on their backs a neat parcel of books. Colin stood up and, holding his head in both hands, staggered into the centre of the narrow street, where the children parted and converged about him. A small girl tossed a tennis ball against his stomach and caught it neatly on the bounce; squeals of glee and congratulation ran through the crowd. Then the chiming ceased, and the remaining children fell silent and began to run grimly. The street was suddenly and conspicuously empty. Mary was bent double by the step, scratching the calf and ankle of one leg vigorously with both hands. Colin stood in the centre of the street, swaying slightly and staring in the direction of the low buildings.

'Something has bitten me,' Mary called.

Colin went and stood behind her and watched as she scratched. A number of small red points were broadening to the size of coins and flushing crimson. 'I wouldn't keep on,' Colin said. He took her wrist and drew her into the street. Far behind them they heard the children, their voices distorted by an acoustic which suggested a room of vast proportions, chanting a religious formula or an arithmetical table.

Mary jigged on her foot. 'Oh God!' she cried, a little self-mocking in her anguish. 'If I don't scratch them I'll die. And I'm so thirsty!'

Through his hangover, Colin had acquired a distant, rough authority, quite untypical. Standing behind Mary, and pinning her hands by her sides, he pointed her down the street. 'If we walk down there,' he said into her ear, 'I think we'll come to the sea. There'll be a café open down there.'

Mary let herself be pushed forwards. 'You haven't shaved.'

'Remember,' Colin said, as they picked up speed down the slope, 'we're on holiday.'

The sea lay immediately beyond the curve in the street.

The frontage was narrow and deserted, bound in both directions by an unbroken line of weather-beaten houses. High poles jutted from the smooth, yellowish water at odd, futile angles, but there were no boats moored to them. On Colin and Mary's right a pitted tin sign pointed the way, along the quayside, to a hospital. A small boy, flanked by two middle-aged women carrying bulging plastic carrier-bags, arrived on the waterfront by the same street as they had. The group stopped by the sign and the women bent down to look through their bags as though something had been forgotten. As they set off, the boy made some piping demand and was instantly hushed.

Colin and Mary sat down near the quay's edge on packing cases which smelled strongly of dead fish. It was a relief to be free of the narrow streets and passageways of the city behind them, to be staring out to sea. The view was dominated by a low, walled island, half a mile out, which was completely given over to a cemetery. At one end was a chapel and a small stone jetty. At this distance, the perspective distorted by a bluish early morning mist, the bright mausoleums and headstones presented the appearance of an overdeveloped city of the future. Behind a low bank of pollution haze, the sun was a disc of dirty silver, small and precise.

Once more Mary leaned against Colin's shoulder. 'You're going to have to look after *me* today.' She spoke through a yawn.

He stroked the nape of her neck. 'Did you look after *me* yesterday then?'

She nodded and closed her eyes. The demand to be looked after was routine between them, and they took it in turns to respond dutifully. Colin cradled Mary in his arms and, somewhat abstractedly, kissed her ear. From behind the cemetery island a water bus had appeared and was moving by the stone jetty. Even at this distance it was possible to see that the tiny figures in black who descended bore flowers. A thin, reedy cry reached them across the water, a gull, or perhaps a child, and the boat edged away from the island.

It was making for the hospital jetty, which lay beyond a bend in the waterfront, out of sight from where they sat. The hospital itself however towered above the surrounding buildings, a citadel of peeling, mustard-yellow distemper, of steep roofs of pale red tiles supporting a tottering mess of television aerials. Some wards had high, barred windows which opened on to balconies the size of small ships where patients, or nurses, dressed in white sat or stood staring out to sea.

The waterfront and the streets behind Colin and Mary were filling with people. Old women in black shawls, wrapped in silence, trudged by with empty shopping bags. From a nearby house came the sharp smell of strong coffee and cigar smoke which mingled with and almost obliterated the odour of dead fish. A wizened fisherman who wore a torn grey suit and a once-white shirt without buttons, as though he had long ago escaped an office job, dropped a pile of nets near the packing cases, almost at their feet. Colin made a vague, apologetic gesture, but the man, who was already walking away, enunciated with precision 'Tourists!' and waved his hand in special dispensation.

Colin woke Mary and persuaded her to walk with him to the hospital jetty. If there were no café there, the water bus would take them through the canals to the centre of town, not so far from their hotel.

By the time they arrived at the imposing gatehouse that was the entrance to the hospital, the water bus was leaving. Two young men in blue jackets, silver-rimmed dark glasses and identical, pencil-thin moustaches operated the boat. One stood ready at the wheel while the other unwound the mooring rope from a bollard with deft, contemptuous turns of the wrist; at the last possible moment he stepped aboard across the widening gap of oily water, released, in the same movement, the steel barrier behind which the passengers crowded, and secured it with one hand while staring impassively at the receding quay and talking loudly to his colleague.

Without discussing the matter, Colin and Mary turned inland and joined the people who streamed through the gatehouse, up a steep driveway lined with flowering shrubs, towards the hospital. Elderly women sat on stools selling magazines, flowers, crucifixes and statuettes, but no one even paused to look.

'If there's an out-patients',' Colin said, tightening his hold on Mary's hand, 'there might be a place selling refreshments.'

Mary was suddenly exasperated; 'I've got to have a glass of water. Surely they'll have that.' Her lower lip was cracked and the skin round her eyes dark.

'Bound to,' Colin said. 'It's a hospital after all.'

A queue had formed outside a set of ornate glass doors which were topped by a great semi-circle of stained glass. By standing on tiptoes they could make out, through the reflections of people and shrubs, a uniformed figure, a porter or a policeman, standing in the gloom between one set of doors and another, examining the credentials of each visitor. All around them people were taking from pockets and handbags their bright yellow card. It was clearly visiting hour in the wards, for none of those waiting appeared to be ill. The crowd edged nearer the door. An elegantly lettered sign propped on an easel announced one long and complex sentence in which a word closely resembling 'security' featured twice. Too tired to detach themselves in time from the queue, or to explain their need for refreshment once they had crossed the threshold and found themselves facing the uniformed guard, Colin and Mary descended the drive once more, pursued by general suggestions from the sympathetic crowd at the door; there appeared to be several cafés in the neighbourhood, but none close by the hospital gates. Mary said she wanted to sit down somewhere and cry, and it was while they were looking about for a suitable spot that they heard a shout and the muffled roar of a marine engine thrown into reverse; another water bus was tying up at the jetty.

To reach the hotel, it was necessary to walk across one of the great tourist attractions of the world, an immense wedge-shaped expanse of paving, enclosed on three sides by dignified arcaded buildings and dominated at its open end by a redbrick clock tower, and beyond that a celebrated cathedral of white domes and glittering façade, a triumphant accretion, so it had often been described, of many centuries of civilization. Assembled on the two longer sides of the square, facing across the paving stones like opposing armies, were the tightly packed ranks of chairs and round tables belonging to the long established cafés; adjacent orchestras, staffed and conducted by men in dinner jackets, oblivious to the morning heat, played simultaneously martial and romantic music, waltzes and extracts from popular operas with thunderous climaxes. Everywhere pigeons banked, strutted and excreted, and each café orchestra paused uncertainly after the earnest, puny applause of its nearest customers. Tourists surged across the brilliantly-lit open ground, or wheeled off in small groups and dissolved into the monochrome patchwork of light and shade within the delicately colonnaded arcades. Two-thirds, perhaps, of the adult males carried cameras.

Colin and Mary had walked with difficulty from the boat and now, before crossing the square, stood in the diminishing shade of the clock tower. Mary took a succession of deep breaths, and over the din suggested that they find a drink of water here. Keeping close together, they set off round the edge of the square, but there were no vacant tables, there were no tables even that could be shared, and it became apparent that much of the movement backwards and forwards across the square consisted of people in search of a place to sit down, and that those who left for the labyrinthine streets did so in exasperation.

Finally, and only by standing several minutes at the table of an elderly couple who writhed in their seats waving their bill, they were able to sit, and then it was obvious that the table was on a remote flank of their waiter's territory, and that many others who craned their necks and snapped their fingers unheard would receive attention before them. Mary gazed at Colin with narrowing bloodshot eyes and muttered something through cracked lips that were beginning to swell; and when he jokingly offered her the slops from the diminutive coffee cup in front of him, she buried her face in her hands.

Colin walked quickly round the tables towards the arcade. But the group of waiters who lounged in deep shade at the entrance to the bar shooed him away. 'No water,' said one, and indicated the bright sea of paying customers framed by the dark curves of the arches. Back at the table, Colin took Mary's hand. They were roughly equidistant from two orchestras, and though the sound was not loud, the dissonances and cross-rhythms made it difficult to decide what to do. 'They're bringing something I think,' Colin said uneasily.

They released their hands and sat back. Colin followed Mary's gaze to a nearby family whose baby, supported at the waist by its father, stood on the table, swaying among the ashtrays and empty cups. It wore a white sun hat, a green-and-white striped matelot vest, bulging pants frilled with pink lace and white ribbon, yellow ankle-socks and scarlet leather shoes. The pale blue circular bits of its dummy pressed tight against and obscured its mouth, giving it an air of sustained, comic surprise. From the corner of its mouth a snail's trail of drool gathered in the deep fold of its chin and overflowed in a bright pendant. The baby's hands clenched and unclenched, its head wobbled quizzically, its fat, weak legs were splayed round the massive, shameless burden of its nappy. The wild eyes, round and pure, blazed across the sunlit square and fixed in seeming astonishment and anger on the roofline of the cathedral where, it had once been written, the crests of the arches, as if in ecstasy, broke into marble foam and tossed themselves far into the blue sky in flashes and wreaths of sculptured spray, as if breakers on a shore had been frost-bound before they fell. The baby emitted a thick, guttural vowel sound and its arms twitched in the direction of the building.

Colin raised his hand tentatively as a waiter whirled towards them bearing a tray of empty bottles; but the man had passed them and was several feet away before the gesture was half-complete. The family was preparing to leave and the infant was handed round until it reached its mother, who wiped its mouth with the back of her hand, placed it carefully on its back in a silver-trimmed pram and set about securing with sharp tugs its arms and chest into a many-buckled leather harness. It lay back and fixed its furious gaze on the sky as it was wheeled away.

'I wonder', Mary said, watching it go, 'how the children are.' Mary's two children were staying with their father who lived on a rural commune. Three postcards, addressed to them and all written on the first day, still lay on the bedside table in the hotel room, without stamps.

'Missing their football, sausages, comics and fizzy drinks, but otherwise fine, is my guess,' Colin said. Two men holding hands, in search of somewhere to sit, stood pressed against their table for a moment.

'All those mountains and wide open spaces,' Mary said. 'You know this place can be terribly suffocating sometimes.' She glared at Colin.

He took her hand. 'We should send those cards.'

Mary pulled her hand away and looked round at the hundreds of feet of repeating arches and columns.

Colin also looked round. There were no waiters in sight and everyone appeared to have a full glass.

'It's like a prison here,' Mary said.

Colin folded his arms and looked at her a long time without blinking. It had been his idea to come. At last he said, 'Our flight is paid for and it doesn't leave for ten days.'

'We could get the train.'

Colin stared past Mary's head.

The two orchestras had stopped at once, and the players were making their way towards the arcades, to the bars of their respective cafés; without their music, the square seemed even more spacious, only partially filled by the sounds of footsteps, the sharp click of smart shoes, the slap of sandals; and voices, murmurs of awe, children's shouts, parental commands of restraint. Mary folded her arms and let her head drop.

Colin stood up and waved both arms at a waiter who nodded and began to move towards them, collecting orders and empty glasses as he came. 'I can't believe it,' Colin cried exultantly.

'We should have brought them with us,' Mary said to her lap.

Colin was still on his feet. 'He's actually coming!' He sat down and tugged at her wrist. 'What would you like?'

'It was mean of us to leave them behind.'

'I think it was rather considerate.'

The waiter, a large, affluent-looking man with a thick, greying beard and gold-rimmed glasses, was suddenly at their table inclining towards them, eyebrows slightly cocked.

'What do you want, Mary?' Colin whispered urgently.

Mary folded her hands in her lap and said, 'A glass of water, without ice.'

'Yes, *two* of those,' Colin said eagerly, 'and . . .'

The waiter straightened and a short hiss escaped his nostrils. 'Water?' he said distantly. His eyes moved between them, appraising their dishevelment. He took a step backwards and nodded towards a corner of the square. 'Is a tap.'

As he began to move away, Colin span round in his chair and caught his sleeve. 'No, but waiter,' he pleaded. 'We also wanted some coffee and some . . .'

The waiter shook his arm free. 'Coffee!' he repeated, his nostrils flared in derision. 'Two coffee?'

'Yes, yes!'

The man shook his head and was gone.

Colin slumped in his chair, closed his eyes and shook his head slowly; Mary struggled to sit up straight.

She kicked his foot gently under the table. 'Come on. It's only ten minutes to the hotel.' Colin nodded but he did not open his eyes. 'We can have a shower, and sit on our balcony and have anything we want brought up to us.' As Colin's chin sank towards his chest, so Mary became more animated. 'We can get into bed. Mmm, those clean white sheets. We'll close the shutters. Can you imagine anything better? We can . . .'

'All right,' Colin said dully. 'Let's walk to the hotel.' But neither of them stirred.

Mary pursed her lips, and then said, 'He's probably bringing the coffee anyway. When people shake their heads, here, it can mean all sorts of things.'

As the morning heat had intensified, the crowds had diminished; there were now sufficient tables, and those who still walked in the square were dedicated sightseers, or citizens with real destinations, all scattered figures who, dwarfed by the immensity of vacant space, shimmered in the warped air. Across the square the orchestra had reassembled and was beginning a Viennese waltz; on Colin and Mary's side, the conductor was leafing through a score, as the musicians were finding their seats and arranging the music on their stands. One consequence of knowing each other so well was that Mary and Colin frequently found themselves staring at the same thing without comment; this time, a man over two hundred feet away with his back to them. His white suit was distinctive in the glare; he had stopped to listen to the waltz. In one hand was a camera, in the other he held a cigarette. He lounged with his weight on one foot and his head moved in time to the simple rhythm. Then he turned suddenly as if bored, for the music had not finished, and sauntered in their direction, dropping his cigarette as he came and treading on it without looking down. From his breast pocket he took, without breaking his stride, a pair of sunglasses which he polished briefly with a white handkerchief before putting on; each of his movements appeared so economical as to be contrived. Despite the sunglasses, the well-cut suit and the pale grey silk tie, they recognized him at once and watched his approach, mesmerized. There was no telling whether he had seen them, but now he was walking directly towards their table.

Colin groaned. 'We should have gone to the hotel.'

We should turn our faces,' Mary said, but they continued to watch as he came closer, compelled by the novelty of recognizing someone in a foreign town, by the fascination of seeing without being seen.

'He's missed us,' Colin whispered, but, as though cued, Robert stopped, took off his glasses, spread his arms wide and called, 'My friends!' and came quickly towards them. 'My friends!' He shook Colin's hand and raised Mary's to his lips.

They sat back and smiled at him weakly. He had found a

chair and was sitting between them, grinning broadly as if several years, rather than a few hours, had passed since they had parted. He was sprawling in his chair, resting his ankle on his knee, revealing soft leather boots of pale cream. The faint scent of his cologne, so different from his perfume of the night before, spread about the table. Mary began to scratch her leg. When they explained that they had not yet been back to the hotel, that they had slept in the street, Robert gasped in horror and sat up straight. Across the square, the first waltz had merged imperceptibly with a second; nearby, the second orchestra launched into a stiff-jointed tango, 'Hernando's Hideaway'.

'This is my fault,' Robert cried. 'I kept you late with wine, and my stupid stories.'

'Stop scratching,' Colin said to Mary; and to Robert: 'Not at all. We should have brought our street maps.'

But already Robert was on his feet, one hand resting on Colin's forearm, the other reaching for Mary's hand. 'Yes, it is my responsibility. I shall make up for everything. You will accept my hospitality.'

'Oh, we couldn't,' Colin said vaguely. 'We're staying at a hotel.'

'When you are so tired, a hotel is not such a good place. I will make you so comfortable you'll forget your terrible night.' Robert pushed his chair in to allow Mary to pass.

Colin tugged at her skirt. 'Wait a minute though . . .' The brief tango jerked to its finale and became, by clever modulation, a Rossini overture; the waltz had become a gallop. Colin stood too, frowning with the effort of concentration. 'Wait . . .'

But Robert was handing Mary through the space between the tables. Her movements had the slow automation of a sleep-walker. Robert turned and called impatiently to Colin. 'We'll take a taxi.'

They walked past the orchestra, past the clock tower,

whose shadow now was no more than a stump, and on to the busy waterfront, the focal point of the teeming lagoon, where the boatmen appeared to recognize Robert immediately and competed ferociously for his custom.

chapter
five

Through the half-open shutters the setting sun cast a
rhomboid of orange bars against the bedroom wall. It was,
presumably, the movement of wisps of cloud that caused the
bars to fade and blur, and then brighten into focus. Mary
had been watching them a full half-minute before she was
fully awake. The room was high-ceilinged, white-walled,
uncluttered; between her bed and Colin's stood a frail
bamboo table which supported a stone pitcher and two
glasses; against the adjacent wall was a carved chest and on
it an earthenware vase in which was arranged, surprisingly,
a sprig of honesty. The dry, silver leaves stirred and rustled
in the warm draughts of air that engulfed the room through
the half-open window. The floor appeared to be constructed
of one unbroken slab of marble of mottled green and brown.
Mary sat up effortlessly and rested her bare feet on its icy
surface. A louvred door, which stood ajar, led into a white
tiled bathroom. Another door, the one through which they
had entered, was closed, and hanging from a brass hook was
a white dressing-gown. Mary poured herself a glass of water,
as she had done several times before falling asleep; this time
she sipped rather than gulped, and sat up very straight,
stretching her spine to its limit, and looked at Colin.

Like her he was naked and lay above the sheets, prone
below the waist, above it twisted a little awkwardly towards
her. His arms were crossed foetally over his chest and his

slender, hairless legs were set a little apart, the feet, abnormally small like a child's, pointing inwards. The fine bones of his spine ran into a deep groove in the small of his back, and along this line, picked out by the low light from the shutters, grew a fine down. Around Colin's narrow waist were little indentations, like teeth marks, in the smooth white skin, caused by the elastic in his pants. His buttocks were small and firm, like a child's. Mary leaned forwards to stroke him and changed her mind. Instead she set her water down on the table and moved closer to examine his face, as one might a statue's.

It was exquisitely made, with an ingenious disregard for the usual proportions. The ear – only one was visible – was large and protruded slightly; the skin was so pale and fine it was almost translucent, and in its interior folded many more times than was common into impossible whorls; the ear lobes too were long, swelling and tapering like tear drops. Colin's eyebrows were thick pencil lines, drooping to the bridge of his nose and almost touching to a point. His eyes, set deep, were dark when open, and now were closed by grey, spiky lashes. In sleep the puzzled frown that rucked his brow, even through laughter, had receded, leaving a barely visible watermark. The nose, like the ears, was long, but in profile it did not protrude; instead it lay flat, along the face, and carved into its base, like commas, were extraordinarily small nostrils. Colin's mouth was straight and firm parted by just a hint of tooth. His hair was unnaturally fine, like a baby's, and black, and fell in curls on to his slender, womanly neck.

Mary crossed to the window and opened the shutters wide. The room faced directly into the setting sun and appeared to be four or five storeys up, higher than most of the surrounding buildings. With such strong light directly into her eyes, it was difficult to discern the pattern of streets below, and to gauge their position relative to the hotel. The mixed sounds of footsteps, television music, the rattle of cutlery and dishes, dogs and innumerable voices rose from the streets as though from a gigantic orchestra and choir. She closed the shutters quietly, restoring the bars to the wall. Attracted by the generous size of the room, the shining, uncluttered marble floor, Mary set about her yoga exercises. Gasping at the coldness of the floor against her buttocks, she sat with her legs stretched out in front of her and her back straight. She leaned forwards slowly, with a long exhalation, reaching for and grasping the soles of her feet in both hands, and lay her trunk along her legs till her head rested on her shins. She remained in this position for several minutes, eyes closed, breathing regularly. When she straightened, Colin was sitting up.

Still dazed, he looked from her empty bed to the pattern on the wall, to Mary on the floor. 'Where are we then?'

Mary lay on her back. 'I'm not sure exactly.'

'Where's Robert?'

'I don't know.' She lifted her legs over her head till they rested on the floor behind her.

Colin stood up, and sat down almost immediately. 'Well, what time is it?'

Mary's voice was muffled. 'Evening.'

'How are your bites?'

'Gone, thanks.'

Colin stood up again, this time carefully, and looked around. He folded his arms. 'What's happened to our clothes?'

Mary said, 'I don't know,' and raised her legs above her head into a shoulder stand.

Colin walked unsteadily to the bathroom door and poked his head in. 'They're not in here.' He picked up the vase of honesty and lifted the lid of the chest. 'Or here.'

'No,' Mary said.

He sat down on his bed and watched her. 'Don't you think we ought to find them? Aren't you worried?'

'I feel good,' Mary said.

Colin sighed. 'Well I'm going to find out what's going on.'

Mary lowered her legs and addressed the ceiling. 'There's a dressing-gown hanging on the door.' She arranged her limbs as comfortably as she could on the floor, turned her palms upwards, closed her eyes and began to breathe deeply through her nose.

Some minutes later she heard Colin, his voice bottled by the acoustics of the bathroom, call testily, 'I can't wear this.' She opened her eyes as he stepped into the room. 'Oh yes!' said Mary wonderingly as she crossed the room. 'You look so lovely.' She pulled his curls free of the frilled collar, and felt for his body beneath the fabric. 'You look like a god. I think I'll have to take you to bed.' She tugged at his arm, but Colin pulled away.

'It's not a dressing-gown anyway,' he said, 'it's a *nightie*.' He pointed to a cluster of flowers embroidered across his chest.

Mary took a pace backwards. 'You've no idea how good you look in it.'

Colin began to take the nightdress off. 'I can't walk around', he said from inside it, 'in a stranger's house dressed like this.'

'Not with an erection,' Mary said as she returned to her yoga. She stood with her feet together and hands by her sides, bent forward to touch her toes, and then doubling even further, placed her hands and wrists flat against the floor.

Colin stood watching her with the nightdress draped over his arm. 'That's good news about your bites,' he said after a while. Mary grunted. When she was upright again he went over to her. 'You'll have to wear it,' he said. 'Go and see what's going on.'

Mary leaped in the air and landed with her feet well apart. She stretched her trunk sideways until she could grasp her left ankle in her left hand. Her right was thrust in the air, and she looked along it, up at the ceiling. Colin dropped the nightie on the floor and lay down on his bed. Fifteen minutes passed before Mary retrieved it and put it on, arranged her hair in the bathroom mirror, and, with a wry smile at Colin, left the room.

She was picking her way slowly through a long gallery of treasures, heirlooms, a family museum in which a minimum of living space had been improvised round the exhibits, all ponderously ornate, unused and lovingly cared-for items of dark mahogany, carved and polished, splay-footed, and cushioned in velvet. Two grandfather clocks stood in a recess on her left, like sentinels, and ticked against each other. Even the smaller objects, stuffed birds in glass domes, vases, fruit bowls, lamp stands, inexplicable brass and cut-glass objects, appeared too heavy to lift, pressed into place by the weight of time and lost histories. A set of three windows along the western wall cast the same orange bars now fading, but here the design was broken by worn patterned rugs. In the centre of the gallery were a large, polished dining-table, with matching high-backed chairs placed around it. At the end of this table were a telephone, a writing pad and a pencil. On the walls hung more than a dozen oil paintings, mostly portraits, a few yellowing landscapes. The portraits were uniformly dark; sombre clothes, muddy backgrounds against which the faces of the subjects glowed like moons. Two landscapes showed leafless trees, barely discernible, towering over dark lakes, on whose shores shadowy figures danced with raised arms.

   At the end of the gallery were two doors, one of which they had entered by; they were disproportionately small, unpanelled and painted white, and the impression they gave was of a grand mansion divided into flats. Mary stopped in front of a sideboard which stood against the wall between

two of the windows, a monstrosity of reflecting surfaces
whose every drawer had a brass knob in the shape of a
woman's head. All the drawers she tried were locked.
Carefully arranged on top was a display of personal but
ostentatious items: a tray of silver-backed men's hair- and
clothes-brushes, a decorated china shaving-bowl, several
cut-throat razors arranged in a fan, a row of pipes in an
ebony rack, a riding crop, a fly swat, a gold tinder-box, a
watch on a chain. On the wall behind this display were
sporting prints, mostly horses racing, their front and back
legs splayed, the riders top-hatted.

Mary had wandered the entire length of the gallery –
making detours round the larger items, stopping to stare into
a gilt-framed mirror – before she was aware of the most
prominent feature. Sliding glass doors on the eastern wall
gave on to a long balcony. From where she stood the light
from the chandeliers made it difficult to see into the semi-
darkness outside, but a great profusion of flowering plants
was just visible, and creepers, small trees in tubs and, Mary
held her breath, a small pale face watching her from the
shadows, a disembodied face, for the night sky and the
room's reflections in the glass made it impossible to see
clothes or hair. It continued to stare at her, unblinking, a
perfectly oval face; then it moved backwards and sideways
into the shadows and disappeared. Mary exhaled noisily.
The reflected room shook as the glass doors opened. A young
woman, her hair tied back severely, stepped a little stiffly
into the room and extended her hand. 'Come outside,' she
said. 'It's pleasanter.'

A few stars had already broken through a sky of bruised
pastels, and yet it was easy enough to make out the sea, the
mooring poles, and even the dark outlines of the cemetery
island. Directly below the balcony, forty feet down, was a
deserted courtyard. The concentrated mass of potted flowers
gave off a penetrating fragrance, almost sickly. The woman

lowered herself into a canvas chair with a little gasp of pain.

'It is beautiful,' she said, as though Mary had spoken. 'I spend as much time as possible out here.' Mary nodded. The balcony extended about half the length of the room. 'My name is Caroline. Robert's wife.'

Mary shook her hand, introduced herself and sat down in a chair facing her. A small white table separated them, and on it was a single biscuit on a plate. In the flowering ivy that covered the wall behind them a cricket was singing. Again, Caroline stared at Mary as though she herself could not be seen; her eyes moved steadily from Mary's hair, to her eyes, to her mouth, and on down to where the table obstructed her view.

'Is it yours?' Mary said, fingering the sleeve of the nightdress.

The question appeared to bring Caroline out of a daydream. She sat up in her chair, folded her hands in her lap and crossed her legs, as though adopting an advised posture for conversation. When she spoke, her tone was forced, pitched a little higher than before. 'Yes, I made it myself sitting out here. I like embroidery.'

Mary complimented her on her work, and there followed a silence in which Caroline appeared to struggle to find something to say. With a nervous start she registered Mary's passing glance at the biscuit and immediately she was holding the plate out to her. 'Please take it.'

'Thank you.' Mary tried to eat the biscuit slowly.

Caroline watched her anxiously. 'You must be hungry. Would you like something to eat?'

'Yes please.'

But Caroline did not stir immediately. Instead she said, 'I'm sorry Robert isn't here. He asked me to apologize. He's gone to his bar. On business, of course. A new manager starts tonight.'

Mary looked up from the empty plate. 'His bar?'

With great difficulty Caroline began to rise, speaking through evident pain. She shook her head when Mary offered help. 'He owns a bar. It's a kind of hobby, I guess. It's the place he took you to.'

'He never mentioned he owned it,' Mary said.

Caroline picked up the plate and walked to the door. When she got there she had to turn her whole body to look at Mary. She said neutrally, 'You know more about it than I do, I've never been there.'

She returned fifteen minutes later with a small wicker basket heaped with sandwiches, and two glasses of orange juice. She edged on to the balcony and allowed Mary to take the tray from her. Mary remained standing while Caroline eased herself into her chair.

'Have you hurt your back?'

But Caroline said simply, pleasantly, 'Eat, and leave some for your friend.' Then she added rapidly, 'Are you fond of your friend?'

'Colin, you mean,' Mary said.

Caroline spoke cautiously, her face tensed as though she expected at any moment a loud explosion. 'I hope you don't mind. There's something I should tell you. It's only fair. You see, I came in and looked at you while you were sleeping. I sat on the trunk about half an hour. I hope you're not angry.'

Mary swallowed and said, uncertainly, 'No.'

Caroline appeared suddenly younger. She played with her fingers like an embarrassed teenager. 'I thought it was better to tell you. I don't want you to feel I was spying on you. You don't think that, do you?'

Mary shook her head. Caroline's voice was barely above a whisper. 'Colin is very beautiful. Robert said he was. You are too, of course.'

Mary continued to eat sandwiches, one after another, her eyes fixed on Caroline's hands.

Caroline cleared her throat. 'I expect you think I'm mad, as well as rude. Are you in love?'

Mary had eaten half the sandwiches and one or two more. 'Well, yes, I do love him, but perhaps you mean something different by "in love".' She looked up. Caroline was waiting for her to go on. 'I'm not obsessed by him, if that's what you mean, by his body, the way I was when I first met him. But I trust him. He's my closest friend.'

Caroline spoke excitedly, more child than teenager. 'By "in love" I mean that you'd do anything for the other person, and . . .' She hesitated. Her eyes were extraordinarily bright. 'And you'd let them do anything to you.'

Mary relaxed in her chair and cradled her empty glass. 'Anything's a rather big word.'

Caroline spoke defiantly. Her small hands were clenched. 'If you are in love with someone, you would even be prepared to let them kill you, if necessary.'

Mary took yet another sandwich. 'Necessary?'

Caroline had not heard. 'That's what I mean by "in love",' she said triumphantly.

Mary pushed the sandwiches out of her own reach. 'And presumably you'd be prepared to kill the person you're "in love" with.'

'Oh yes, if I was the man I would.'

'The man?'

But Caroline lifted her forefinger theatrically and cocked her head. 'I heard something,' she whispered, and began to struggle out of her chair.

The door swung open and Colin stepped rather cautiously on to the balcony, holding a small white hand towel round his waist.

'This is Caroline, Robert's wife,' Mary said. 'This is Colin.'

When they shook hands, Caroline's gaze was fixed on Colin the way it had been on Mary. Colin's was on the remaining sandwiches. 'Pull up a chair,' Caroline said, indicating a folding canvas chair further along the balcony. Colin sat down between them with his back to the sea, and one hand on his waist to keep his towel in place. Watched closely by Caroline, he ate the sandwiches. Mary turned her chair away a little so she could watch the sky. For a while no one spoke. Colin finished his orange juice and tried to catch Mary's eye. Then Caroline, again self-consciously conversational, asked Colin if he was enjoying his stay. 'Yes,' he answered, and smiled at Mary, 'except we keep getting lost.'

There followed another short silence. Then Caroline made them jump by exclaiming loudly, 'Of course! Your clothes. I forgot. I washed and dried them. They're in the locked cupboard in your bathroom.'

Mary did not take her eyes off the multiplying stars. 'That was very kind of you.'

Caroline smiled at Colin. 'You know, I thought you'd turn out to be a quiet sort of person.'

Colin tried to rearrange his towel across his lap. 'You heard of me before then?'

'Caroline came in and watched us while we were asleep,' Mary explained, her tone carefully level.

'Are you an American?' Colin inquired politely.

'Canadian, please.'

Colin nodded briskly, as though the difference was significant.

Caroline suppressed a giggle, and held up a small key. 'Robert is very keen for you to stop and have dinner with us. He told me not to let you have your clothes until you'd agreed.' Colin laughed politely and Mary stared while Caroline swung the key between her forefinger and thumb. 'Well, I'm very hungry,' Colin said, looking at Mary who said to Caroline, 'I prefer to have my clothes first, and then decide.'

'That's exactly what I think, but Robert insisted.' She became suddenly serious and, leaning forward, placed her hand on Mary's arm. 'Please say you'll stay. We get so few visitors.' She was pleading with them, her eyes moving between Colin's face and Mary's. 'I'd be so happy if you said yes. We eat very well here, I promise you.' And then she added, 'If you don't stay Robert will blame me. Please say yes.'

'Come on, Mary,' Colin said. 'Let's stay.'

'Please!' There was ferocity in Caroline's voice. Mary looked up startled and the two women stared across the table at each other. Mary nodded, and Caroline, exclaiming with delight, tossed the key to her.

chapter
six

The furthest stars of the Milky Way were visible, not as a scattering of fine dust, but as distinct points of light which made the brighter constellations appear uncomfortably close. The very darkness was tangible, warm and cloying. Mary clasped her hands behind her head and watched the sky, and Caroline sat forward eagerly, her gaze moving proudly between Mary's face and the heavens, as though she were personally responsible for their grandeur. 'I spend hours out here.' She seemed to wheedle for praise, but Mary did not even blink.

Colin took the key from the table and stood up. 'I'd feel better', he said, 'if I was wearing more than this.' He gathered up the little towel where it had exposed his thigh.

When he had gone Caroline said, 'Isn't it sweet, when men are shy?'

Mary remarked on the clarity of the stars, on how rarely one saw a night sky from a city. Her tone was deliberate and even.

Caroline sat still, appearing to wait for the last echoes of small talk to fade completely before saying, 'How long have you known Colin?'

'Seven years,' Mary said, and without turning towards Caroline, went on to describe how her children, whose sexes, ages and names she explained in rapid parentheses, were both fascinated by stars, how they could name over a dozen constellations while she could name only one, Orion, whose giant form now straddled the sky before them, his sheathed sword as bright as his far-flung limbs.

Caroline glanced briefly at that portion of sky, and placed her hand on Mary's wrist and said, 'You make a very striking pair, if you don't mind me saying. Both so finely built, almost like twins. Robert says you aren't married. Do you live together then?'

Mary folded her arms and looked at Caroline at last. 'No, we don't.'

Caroline had withdrawn her hand and stared at where it lay in her lap as though it were no longer her own. Her small face, made so geometrically oval by the surrounding darkness and the arrangement of her drawn-back hair, was featureless in its regularity, innocent of expression, without age. Her eyes, nose, mouth, skin, all might have been designed in committee to meet the barest requirements of feasibility. Her mouth, for example, was no more than the word suggested, a moving, lipped slit beneath her nose. She glanced up from her lap and found herself staring into Mary's eyes; she let her gaze fall instantly to the ground between them and continued her questions as before. 'And what do you do, for a living I mean.'

'I used to work in the theatre.'

'An actress!' This idea stirred Caroline. She bent awkwardly in her chair, as though it pained her to keep her back straight, or to relax it.

Mary was shaking her head. 'I was working for a women's theatre group. We did quite well for three years, and now we've broken up. Too many arguments.'

Caroline was frowning, 'Women's theatre? ... Only actresses?'

'Some of us wanted to bring in men, at least from time to time. The others wanted to keep it the way it was, pure. That's what broke us up in the end.'

67

'A play with only women? I don't understand how that could work. I mean, what could *happen*?'

Mary laughed. 'Happen?' she repeated. 'Happen?'

Caroline was waiting for an explanation. Mary lowered her voice, and spoke with her hand partly covering her mouth as though to erase a smile. 'Well, you could have a play about two women who have only just met sitting on a balcony talking.'

Caroline brightened. 'Oh yes. But they're probably waiting for a man.' She glanced at her wrist-watch. 'When he arrives they'll stop talking and go indoors. Something will happen . . .' Caroline was suddenly convulsed by giggles; it would have been laughter if she had not suppressed it so firmly; she steadied herself against the chair, and attempted to keep her mouth closed. Mary nodded seriously and averted her eyes. Then, with a sharp intake of breath, Caroline was still again.

'Well anyway,' Mary said, 'I'm out of a job.'

Caroline was twisting her spine this way and that; all positions seemed to pain her. Mary asked if she could fetch a cushion, but Caroline shook her head curtly, and said, 'It hurts when I laugh.' When Mary asked the cause of the trouble, Caroline shook her head and closed her eyes.

Mary returned to her former position, and looked at the stars and the lights of the fishing boats. Caroline inhaled noisily and rapidly through her nose. Then, after several minutes, when she was breathing more easily, Mary said, 'You're right in a way, of course. Most of the best parts are written for men, on stage and off. We played men when we needed to. It worked best in cabaret, when we were sending them up. We even did an all-woman *Hamlet* once. It was quite a success.'

'Hamlet?' Caroline said the word as if it were new to her. She glanced over her shoulder. 'I never read it. I haven't seen a play since I was at school.' As she spoke more lights came on in the gallery behind them, and the balcony was suddenly illuminated through the glass doors, and divided by lines of deep shadow. 'Isn't it the one with the ghost?' Mary nodded. She was listening to footsteps which had passed the length of the gallery, and which now stopped abruptly. She did not turn round to look. Caroline was watching her. 'And someone locked up in a convent?'

Mary shook her head. The footsteps started, and stopped immediately. A chair scraped and there was a succession of metallic sounds such as cutlery makes. 'There is a ghost,' she said vaguely. 'And a convent, but we never see it.'

Caroline was struggling out of her chair. She was just on her feet as Robert stepped neatly before them and made a little bow. Caroline gathered up the tray and edged past him. They exchanged no greetings, and Robert did not step aside for her. He was smiling at Mary, and they both listened to the irregular steps recede across the gallery floor. A door opened and closed and all was silent.

Robert was wearing the clothes they had seen him in the night before, and the same piercing aftershave. A trick of shadow made him seem even squatter. He put his hands behind his back and, taking a couple of paces towards Mary, inquired politely whether she and Colin had slept well. There followed a succession of pleasantries: Mary admired the flat, and the view from the balcony; Robert explained that the whole house had once belonged to his grandfather, and that when he inherited it he had divided it into five luxury flats, and now lived off the income. He pointed to the cemetery island and said that his grandfather and father were buried there, side by side. Then Mary, indicating the cotton nightdress, stood up and said she felt she ought to dress. He handed her through the door, and guided her towards the great dining-room table, insisting that first she drink a glass of champagne with him. Four deep glasses on tall, pink-tinted stems were arranged on a silver tray around the champagne bottle. Just then Colin appeared through the bedroom door at the far end of the gallery, and walked towards them. They stood at the corner of the table and watched as he approached.

Colin was renewed. He had shampooed his hair and shaved. His clothes were cleaned and ironed. His spotless white shirt had received special attention, and fitted him like never before. His black jeans clung to his legs like tights. He walked towards them slowly, with an embarrassed smile, conscious of their attention. His curls were dark and shone under the chandeliers.

'You look well,' Robert said when Colin was still several feet away, and added frankly, 'Like an angel.'

Mary was grinning. From the kitchen came the clatter of plates. She repeated Robert's sentence softly, stressing each word. 'You . . . look . . . well,' and took his hand. Colin laughed.

Robert released the cork and as the white foam burst from the bottle's narrow neck, he turned his head to one side and called Caroline's name sharply. She appeared immediately at one of the white doors, and took her place at Robert's side, facing the guests. As they raised their glasses she said quietly, 'To Colin and Mary', emptied her glass in rapid gulps, and returned to the kitchen.

Mary excused herself and, as soon as the doors at each end of the gallery had closed, Robert refilled Colin's glass and steered him gently by the elbow round the furniture to a place where they could walk the gallery's length unimpeded. Without quite releasing Colin's elbow, Robert explained various aspects of his father's and grandfather's possessions; a famous cabinet-maker had constructed this priceless corner table with its unique inlay – they had stopped in front of it, and Robert ran his hand over its surface – for his grandfather in return for a legal service that had rescued the reputation of the craftsman's daughter; how the murky paintings on the wall – first collected by his grandfather – were connected with certain famous schools, and how it had been shown by his father that certain brushstrokes were undeniably those of a master, no doubt shaping the course of an acolyte's work. This – Robert had picked up a small, grey replica of a famous cathedral – was made of lead from a unique mine in Switzerland. Colin had to hold the model in two hands. Robert's grandfather, he learned, had several shares in the mine, which was soon exhausted but whose lead was unlike any other in the world. The statuette, formed from one of the last pieces to be dug from the mine, had been commissioned by his father. They moved on, Robert's hand touching, but not quite gripping, Colin's elbow. This was grandfather's seal, these were his opera glasses, also used by father, through which both men had witnessed the first nights of, or the memorable performances of – and here Robert listed several operas, sopranos and tenors. Colin nodded and, initially at least, prompted him with interested questions. But it was not necessary. Robert was guiding him towards a small, carved mahogany bookcase. It held father's and grandfather's favourite novels. All these books were first editions and bore the mark of a distinguished bookseller. Did Colin know the shop? Colin said he had heard of the place. Robert had brought him to the sideboard against the wall between two windows. Robert set down his glass and let his hands drop to his sides. He stood in silence, head bowed as if in prayer. Respectfully, Colin stood a few feet off and regarded the objects which suggested a memory game played at children's parties.

Robert cleared his throat and said: 'These are things my father used every day.' He paused; Colin watched him anxiously. 'Small things.' Once again a silence; Colin combed his hair with his fingers and Robert stared intently at the brushes, pipes and razors.

When at last they moved on Colin said lightly, 'Your father is very important to you.' They arrived once more at the dining-table, by the champagne bottle which Robert emptied into their glasses. Then he ushered Colin towards one of the leather armchairs, but he himself remained standing in such a way that Colin had to turn uncomfortably into the light of the chandelier to see his face.

Robert adopted the tone of one who explains the self-obvious to a child. 'My father and his father understood themselves clearly. They were men, and they were proud of their sex. Women understood them too.' Robert emptied his glass and added, 'There was no confusion.'

'Women did as they were told,' Colin said, squinting into the light.

Robert made a small movement of his hand towards Colin. 'Now men doubt themselves, they hate themselves, even more than they hate each other. Women treat men like children, because they can't take them seriously.' Robert sat on the arm of the chair and rested his hand on Colin's shoulder. His voice dropped. 'But they love men. Whatever they might say they believe, women love aggression and strength and power in men. It's deep in their minds. Look at all the women a successful man attracts. If what I'm saying wasn't true, women would protest at every war. Instead, they love to send their men to fight. The pacifists, the objectors, are mostly men. And even though they hate themselves for it, women long to be ruled by men. It's deep in their minds. They lie to themselves. They talk of freedom, and dream of captivity.' Robert was massaging Colin's shoulder gently as he spoke, Colin sipped his champagne and stared in front of him. Robert's voice now had something of the quality of recital, like a child at its multiplication tables. 'It is the world that shapes people's minds. It is men who have shaped the world. So women's minds are shaped by men. From earliest childhood, the world they see is made by men. Now the women lie to themselves and there is confusion and unhappiness everywhere. It wasn't the case in my grandfather's day. These few things of his remind me of that.'

Colin cleared his throat. 'Your grandfather's day had suffragettes. And I don't understand what bothers you. Men still govern the world.'

Robert laughed indulgently. 'But badly. They don't believe in themselves as men.'

The smell of garlic and frying meat was filling the room. From Colin's gut there came a prolonged and distant sound, like a voice on the telephone. He eased himself forward, out from under Robert's hand. 'So,' he said as he stood up, 'this is a museum dedicated to the good old days.' His voice was affable, but strained.

Robert stood up too. The geometric lines of his face had deepened and his smile was glassy, fixed. Colin had turned back momentarily to set down his empty glass on the arm of the chair, and as he straightened Robert struck him in the stomach with his fist, a relaxed, easy blow which, had it not instantly expelled all the air from Colin's lungs, might have seemed playful. Colin jack-knifed to the floor at Robert's feet where he writhed, and made laughing noises in his throat as he fought for air. Robert took the empty glasses to the table. When he returned he helped Colin to his feet, and made him bend at the waist and straighten several times. Finally Colin broke away and walked about the room taking deep breaths. Then he took out a handkerchief and dabbed at his eyes and glared blearily across the furniture at Robert who was lighting a cigarette and walking towards the kitchen door. Before he reached it he turned and winked at Colin.

Colin sat in a corner of the room and watched Mary help Caroline set the table. Mary glanced at him worriedly from time to time. Once, she crossed the room and squeezed his hand. Robert did not appear until the first course was on the table. He had changed into a pale cream suit and wore a thin black satin tie. They ate a clear soup, steak, green salad and bread. There were two bottles of red wine. They sat at one end of the dining-table, close together, Caroline and Colin on one side, Robert and Mary on the other. In response to Robert's questions Mary talked about her children. Her ten-year-old daughter had finally been selected for the school football team, and had been so savagely tackled by the boys in her first two matches that she had had to spend a week in bed. Then she cut her hair for the next match to avoid persecution and had even scored a goal. Her son, two and a half years younger, could run round the local athletics track in less than ninety seconds. When she had finished explaining all this, Robert, clearly bored, nodded to himself and turned his attention to his food.

There was a prolonged silence at the very heart of the meal, broken only by the sound of cutlery against plates. Then Caroline asked a nervous, complicated question about the children's school which obliged Mary to talk at length about recently-enacted legislation, and the collapse of a movement for reform. When she appealed to Colin for corroboration, he answered in the briefest possible way; and when Robert leaned across the table, touched Colin's arm and pointed to his nearly empty glass, he looked away, over Caroline's head towards a bookcase piled with newspapers and magazines. Mary broke off suddenly and apologized for talking too much, but there was irritation in her voice. Robert smiled at her and took her hand. At the same time he sent Caroline into the kitchen for coffee.

Still holding Mary's hand, he turned his smile to include Colin. 'Tonight there is a new manager starting work in my bar.' He raised his glass. 'To my new manager.'

74

'To your new manager,' Mary said. 'What happened to the old one?'

Colin had picked up his glass but had not raised it. Robert watched him intently, and when at last Colin drank, Robert said, as though teaching etiquette to a simpleton, 'To Robert's new manager'. He filled Colin's glass and turned to Mary. 'The old manager was old, and now he is in trouble with the police. The new manager . . .' Robert pursed his lips and with a quick glance at Colin made a tense little circle with his forefinger and thumb '. . . he knows how to deal with trouble. He knows when to act. He doesn't let people take advantage of him.' Colin held Robert's stare for a moment.

'He sounds just your man,' Mary said politely.

Robert nodded and smiled at her in triumph. '*Just* my man,' he said, and released her hand.

When Caroline returned with the coffee she found Colin sprawled on a chaise-longue, and Robert and Mary talking quietly at the dining-table. She brought Colin his cup and lowered herself beside him, wincing as she did so and holding on to his knee for support. With a quick glance over her shoulder towards Robert, she began to ask Colin about his work and family background, but from the manner in which her eyes roved across his face as he talked, her readiness with fresh questions, it was clear that she was not quite listening to him. She appeared greedy for the fact of conversation rather than its content; she inclined her head towards him, as though bathing her face in the flow of his speech. Despite this, perhaps because of it, Colin spoke easily, first of his failure to become a singer, then of his first acting job, then of his family. 'Then my father died,' he concluded, 'and my mother remarried.'

Caroline was framing another question, but this time hesitantly. Behind her at the table Mary was yawning and standing up. 'Will you . . .' Caroline stopped, and started again. 'You go home soon, I suppose.'

'Next week.'

'Will you come again.' She touched his arm. 'Will you promise to come again.'

Colin was polite and vague. 'Yes of course.'

But Caroline was insistent; 'No, I mean it, it's very important.' Mary was coming towards them, and Robert too was standing up. Caroline lowered her voice. 'I can't walk down stairs.'

Mary stood before them, but hearing Caroline whisper, she moved on towards the bookcase and picked up a magazine. 'Perhaps we should leave,' she called.

Colin nodded gratefully and was about to stand when Caroline took his arm and said quietly, 'I can't get out.'

Robert had joined Mary at the bookcase and they were looking at a large photograph. She took it in her hands. A man stood on a balcony smoking a cigarette. The print was grainy and indistinct, taken from some distance and enlarged many times. He let her hold it a few seconds, then he took it from her and returned it to the bookcase.

Colin and Caroline stood up, and Robert opened the door and turned on the light above the stairs. Colin and Mary thanked Robert and Caroline for their hospitality. Robert gave Mary instructions how to reach the hotel.

'Remember . . .' Caroline said to Colin, but the rest of her words were cut off as Robert closed the door. As they descended the first flight of stairs, they heard a sharp sound that, as Mary said later, could as easily have been an object dropped as a face slapped. They reached the bottom of the stairs, crossed a small courtyard and stepped out into the unlit street. 'Now,' Colin said, 'which way?'

chapter
seven

During the next four days Colin and Mary did not leave the
hotel except to cross the busy thoroughfare and take a table
on the café pontoon which was in sunlight two hours before
their own balcony. They ate all their meals in the hotel, in
the cramped dining-room where the starched white
tablecloths, and even the food, were stained yellow and
green by coloured glass in the windows. The other guests
were friendly and curious, leaning politely towards each
other's tables, comparing notes on the less obvious churches,
on an altar-piece by a more wayward member of a respected
school, on a restaurant used only by locals.

Walking back from the apartment to the hotel, they had
held hands all the way; that night they had slept in the same
bed. They woke surprised to find themselves in each other's
arms. Their lovemaking surprised them too, for the great,
enveloping pleasure, the sharp, almost painful, thrills were
sensations, they said that evening on the balcony, they
remembered from seven years before, when they had first
met. How could they have forgotten so easily? It was over in
less than ten minutes. They lay face to face a long while,
impressed and a little moved. They went into the bathroom
together. They stood under the shower giggling and soaped
each other's body. Thoroughly cleansed and perfumed, they
returned to bed and made love till noon. Hunger drove them
downstairs to the tiny dining-room where the earnest

conversation of the other guests made them titter like school-children. They ate three main courses between them and shared three litres of wine. They held hands across the table and talked about parents and childhood as if they had just met. The other guests glanced at them approvingly. After a three and a half hour absence, they returned to their bed which now had clean sheets and pillowcases. While they were fondling each other they fell asleep, and when they woke in the early evening they repeated the brief, startling experience of that morning. They showered together again, this time without soap, and listened entranced to the man across the courtyard, also showering and singing his aria, *Mann and Weib, und Weib und Mann*. Aperitifs were brought to their room on a tray; fine slices of lemon were arranged on a silver dish, and there was ice stacked in a silver tumbler. They took their drinks on to the balcony where they leaned on the wall lined with geraniums, smoking a joint and watching the sunset and the passers-by.

Thus the pattern, with minor variations, was set for three days. Though they stared across the water at the large church, and mentioned from time to time the name of a restaurant given to them by friends at home, or in the heat of midday evoked the shadowy coolness of a certain street which ran along a neglected canal, they made no serious attempt to leave the hotel. On the afternoon of the second day they dressed for an expedition, but fell on to the bed, pulling at each other's clothes, and laughing at their hopelessness. They sat on the balcony late into the night, with bottles of wine, in the light of the neon sign which obliterated the stars, and talked again of childhood, sometimes remembering events for the first time, formulating theories about the past and about memory itself; each let the other talk for as long as an hour without interrupting. They celebrated their mutual understanding, and the fact that despite their familiarity with each other, they could still recover such passion. They congratulated themselves. They wondered at and described this passion; it meant more than it could have seven years before. They listed their friends, married and unmarried couples; none seemed quite so successfully in love as they were. They did not discuss their stay with Robert and Caroline. Their only references were in passing: 'On the way back from Robert's flat I thought . . .' or 'I was looking at the stars from that balcony . . .'

Their talk turned to orgasms, and to whether men and women experience a similar, or radically different, sensation; radically different, they agreed, but was this difference culturally induced? Colin said that he had long envied women's orgasms, and that there were times when he felt an aching emptiness, close to desire, between his scrotum and his anus; he thought this might be an approximation of womanly desire. Mary described, and they both derided, an experiment reported by a newspaper, the purpose of which was to answer this very question, did men and women feel the same. Volunteers of both sexes were given a list of two hundred phrases, adjectives and adverbs, and asked to ring the ten that best described their experience of orgasm. A second group was asked to look at the results and guess the sex of each volunteer, and since they made as many correct as incorrect identifications, it was concluded that men and women feel the same. They moved on, inevitably, to the politics of sex and talked, as they had many times before, of patriarchy which, Mary said, was the most powerful single principle of organization shaping institutions and individual lives. Colin argued, as he always did, that class dominance was more fundamental. Mary shook her head, but they battled to find common ground.

They returned to their parents; which of the mothers', which of the fathers' characteristics they had acquired: how the relationship between mother and father exerted its influence on their own lives, on their own relationships. The word 'relationship' was on their lips so frequently they sickened of it. They agreed there was no reasonable substitute. Mary talked of herself as a parent, Colin talked of himself as a pseudo-parent to Mary's children; all speculation, all anxieties and memories were marshalled into the service of theories about their own and each other's character as if, finding themselves reborn through an unexpected passion, they had to invent themselves anew, name themselves as a newborn child, or a new character, a sudden intruder in a novel, is named. At various times they returned to the subject of ageing; of the sudden (or was it gradual?) discovery that they were no longer the youngest adults they knew, that their bodies were heavier, no longer self-regulating mechanisms that could be ignored, but rather must be watched closely and consciously exercised. They agreed that while this idyll rejuvenated them, they were not deluded; they agreed they were growing older and one day would die, and these mature reflections, they thought, gave that passion an added profundity.

In fact it was agreement that enabled them to move through so many topics with such patience, that caused them to be still talking in low voices on the balcony at four in the morning, the polythene bag of marihuana, the Rizla packets and the empty wine bottles at their feet; agreement not simply as a consequence of their respective states of mind, but as a rhetorical mode, a means of proceeding. The unspoken assumption in previous conversations about important matters (and these, over the years, had, of course, occurred less frequently) was that a subject was best explored by taking the opposing view, even if it was not quite the view one held oneself; a considered opinion was less important than the fact of opposition. The idea, if it was an idea and not a habit of mind, was that adversaries, fearing contradiction, would be more rigorous in argument, like scientists proposing innovation to their colleagues. What

80

tended to happen, to Colin and Mary at least, was that subjects were not explored so much as defensively reiterated, or forced into elaborate irrelevancies, and suffused with irritability. Now, freed by mutual encouragement they roamed, like children at seaside rockpools, from one matter to another.

But for all this discussion, this analysis which extended to the very means of discussion itself, they could not talk about the cause of their renewal. Their conversation, in essence, was no less celebratory than their lovemaking; in both they lived inside the moment. They clung to each other, in talk as in sex. In the shower they joked about handcuffing themselves together and throwing away the key. The idea aroused them. Without wasting time on towels or on shutting off the water, they ran back to bed to consider it in greater depth. They took to muttering in each other's ear as they made love, stories that came from nowhere, out of the dark, stories that produced moans and giggles of hopeless abandon, that won from the spellbound listener consent to a lifetime of subjection and humiliation. Mary muttered her intention of hiring a surgeon to amputate Colin's arms and legs. She would keep him in a room in her house, and use him exclusively for sex, sometimes lending him out to friends. Colin invented for Mary a large, intricate machine, made of steel, painted bright red and powered by electricity; it had pistons and controls, straps and dials, and made a low hum when it was switched on. Colin hummed in Mary's ear. Once Mary was strapped in, fitted to tubes that fed and evacuated her body, the machine would fuck her, not just for hours or weeks, but for years, on and on, for the rest of her life, till she was dead and on even after that, till Colin, or his solicitor, switched it off.

Afterwards, once they were showered and perfumed and sat sipping their drinks on the balcony, staring over the geranium pots at the tourists in the street below, their muttered stories seemed quite tasteless, silly, and they did not really talk about them.

Through the warm nights, in the narrow single bed, their most characteristic embrace in sleep was for Mary to put her arms round Colin's neck, and Colin his arms round Mary's waist, and for their legs to cross. Throughout the day, even when all subjects and all desire were momentarily exhausted, they stayed close, sometimes stifled by the very warmth of the other's body, but unable to break away for a minute, as though they feared that solitude, private thoughts, would destroy what they shared.

It was not an unreasonable fear. On the morning of the fourth day, Mary woke before Colin and eased herself carefully out of the bed. She washed and dressed quickly, and while her movements were not stealthy, they were not careless either; when she opened the door of their room it was a smooth, co-ordinated action, not the customary flick of the wrist. Outside it was cooler than was usual at ten-thirty, and the air was exceptionally clear; the sun appeared to sculpt objects in fine detail, and set them off with the darkest shadows. Mary crossed the pavement to the pontoon and took a table on its furthest edge, nearest the water and in full sunlight. Her bare arms felt cold however, and she shivered a little as she put on her dark glasses and looked round for a waiter. She was the café's only customer, perhaps its first for the day.

A waiter parted the beaded walk-through of a door across the pavement and indicated that he had seen her. He stepped out of sight and reappeared a little later, walking towards her with a tray on which there was a large, steaming mug. When he set it down, he made it clear that it was on the house and, though Mary would have preferred coffee to hot chocolate, she accepted it gratefully. The waiter smiled and turned briskly on his heel. Mary turned her chair a little inland so she could look towards the balcony and the shuttered windows of their room. Not far from her feet water lapped soothingly against the rubber tyres that protected the pontoon from the iron barges when they moored. Within ten minutes, as though encouraged by her presence there, customers had occupied a few more tables and now her own waiter was joined by another and both were kept busy.

She drank her hot chocolate and looked across the channel to the great church on the other side and the houses packed around it. Occasionally a car on the quayside caught the morning sun on its windscreen and signalled it back across the water. It was too distant to make out people. Then, as she set down her empty cup on the table, she looked round and saw Colin fully dressed on the balcony, smiling at her across a distance of some sixty feet. Mary returned his smile warmly, but when Colin shifted his position a little, as though stepping around something at his feet, her smile froze, and then faded. She looked down puzzled, and glanced over her shoulder across the water again. Two rowing-boats were passing, and their occupants were calling excitedly to one another. Mary looked towards the balcony, and was able to smile again, but once Colin had gone inside, and in the few seconds she had to herself before he joined her, she stared unseeing at the distant quayside, her head cocked, as though struggling, without success, with her memory. When Colin came they kissed and sat close, and remained there two hours.

The rest of the day followed the pattern of the preceding three: they left the café and returned to their room which the maid had just finished tidying. They met her as she was coming out, under one arm a bundle of dirty sheets and pillowcases, in the other hand a wastepaper basket half-full of used paper tissues, and cuttings from Colin's toenails. To

83

let her pass they had to press themselves against the wall, and they turned a little shamefacedly into her polite good morning. They remained in bed less than an hour, spent two hours over lunch, returned to bed, this time to sleep, made love when they woke, lay about for some time afterwards, showered, dressed and spent the rest of the evening, before and after dinner, sitting on their balcony. For all this Mary appeared troubled, and Colin remarked on it several times. She agreed there was something, but it was at the back of her mind, just beyond her reach, she explained, like a vivid dream that cannot be recalled. In the evening they decided they were suffering from lack of exercise and made plans to catch the boat across the lagoon the next day to the popular strip of land whose beaches faced the open sea. This led them to talk at length and euphorically, for they had just smoked another joint, about swimming, their preferred strokes, the relative merits of rivers, lakes, swimming-pools and seas, and the precise nature of the attraction water had for people; was it buried memory of ancient sea ancestors? Talk of memory caused Mary to frown again. The conversation became desultory after that, and they went to bed earlier than usual, a little before midnight.

At half-past five the following morning Mary woke with a shout, perhaps the last of several, and sat upright in bed. The first light of day was penetrating the shutters, and one or two paler objects were visible. From the room next door to theirs came the murmur of a voice and the sound of a light switch. Mary clasped her knees and began to tremble.

Colin was fully awake by now. He reached up and stroked her back. 'A nightmare?' he said. Mary recoiled from his touch, her back tensed. When he touched her again, this time on the shoulder as if to pull her back down beside him, she wrenched free and got out of bed.

Colin sat up. Mary was at the head of the bed staring at

the indentation in Colin's pillow. There were footsteps across the nearby room, a door opened, and footsteps again in the corridor, which broke off abruptly as if to listen.

'What is it, Mary?' Colin said, and reached for her hand. She shrank away, but her eyes were on him, her look startled and remote, as though witnessing a catastrophe from a hilltop. Unlike Mary, Colin was naked, and he shivered as he fumbled for his shirt and stood up. They faced each other across the empty bed. 'You've had a bad fright,' Colin said, and began to edge round towards her. Mary nodded and moved towards the french window that gave on to the balcony. The footsteps outside their room receded, a door closed, bedsprings creaked and a light switch clicked. Mary opened the window and stepped out.

Colin dressed quickly and followed her. She raised a finger to her lips when he began to say comforting things and ask questions. She pushed a low table to one side and gestured at Colin to come and stand in its place. Still asking questions, Colin allowed himself to be positioned. She turned him so he faced across the channel, towards that part of the sky still in night, and she lifted his left hand so it rested on the balcony wall; the light she raised to his face and asked him to hold it there. Then she took a few paces back. 'You're very beautiful, Colin,' she whispered.

A sudden and simple idea appeared to seize him and he turned abruptly. 'You are awake, aren't you, Mary?'

He stepped towards her and this time, instead of backing away, she leaped forward and threw her arms around his neck, and kissed his face and head with desperate repetition. 'I'm so frightened. I love you and I'm so frightened,' she cried. Her body grew tauter and shook till her teeth chattered and she could no longer speak.

'What is it, Mary?' Colin said quickly, and embraced her hard. She was tugging at his shirt sleeve, trying to push his

85

arm down. 'You're not properly awake, are you? You had a bad dream.'

'Touch me,' Mary said at last. 'Just touch me.'

Colin pulled clear of her and shook her shoulders gently. His voice was hoarse. 'You've got to tell me what's happening.'

Mary was suddenly calmer, and allowed herself to be led back indoors. She stood watching while Colin re-made the bed. As they got in she said, 'I'm sorry I frightened you,' and kissed him, guiding his hand between her thighs.

'Not now,' Colin said. 'Tell me what happened.'

She nodded and lay down, her head pillowed on his arm. 'I'm sorry,' she said again after several minutes.

'What happened then?' He spoke through a yawn, and Mary did not reply immediately.

A boat throbbed soothingly up the channel towards the docks. When it had passed Mary said, 'I woke up and realized something. If I'd realized it in the daytime I wouldn't have been so frightened by it.'

'Ah,' said Colin.

Mary waited. 'Don't you want to know what it was?' Colin mumbled assent. Again Mary paused. 'Are you awake?'

'Yes.'

'That photograph at Robert's is of you.'

'What photograph?'

'I saw a photograph at Robert's flat, and it was of you.'

'Me?'

'It must have been taken from a boat, a little way beyond the café.'

Colin's leg twitched violently. 'I don't remember that,' he said, after a pause.

'You're falling asleep,' Mary said. 'Try and stay awake a moment.'

86

'I am awake.'

'When I was down at the café this morning I saw you on the balcony. I couldn't work it out. Then I woke up and remembered. Robert showed me that photograph. Colin? Colin?'

He lay perfectly still and his breathing was barely audible.

chapter
eight

Although it was their hottest day so far, and the sky directly above was closer to black than blue, the sea, when they finally came to it down the busy avenue of street cafés and souvenir shops, was an oily grey along whose surface the gentlest of breezes pushed and scattered patches of off-white foam. At the water's edge, where miniature waves broke on to the straw-coloured sand, children played and shouted. Further out there was the occasional swimmer lifting arm over arm in solemn exercise, but most of the vast crowd which stretched away to the left and right into the heat haze had come to sun itself. Large families sat round trestle tables preparing lunches of bright green salads and dark bottles of wine. Solitary men and women flattened themselves on towels, their bodies iridescent with oil. Transistor radios played and now and then there could be heard, above the babble of children playing, the falling sound of a parent calling a child's name.

Colin and Mary walked for two hundred yards over the hot, heavy sand, past lonely men with cigarettes and paperback books, past love affairs and through households with grandparents and hot babies in prams, looking for the exact place, near the water, but not too near the splashing children, away from the nearest transistor, and the family with two energetic Alsatian dogs, not too close to violate the privacy of the oiled couple on a pink towel, or to the concrete waste bin above which danced a thick cloud of blue-black flies. Each potential location was disqualified on at least one count. One empty space was suitable but for the litter scattered around its centre. Five minutes later they returned to it and began to carry the empty bottles and cans and half-eaten pieces of bread to the concrete dustbin, but a man and his son, their black hair sleeked back with water, ran out of the sea and insisted that their picnic remain untouched. Colin and Mary walked on and agreed – this was their first conversation since stepping off the boat – that what they really had in mind was a beach which approximated, as far as possible, the privacy of their hotel room.

They settled at last near two teenage girls whom a small knot of men were trying to impress by turning clumsy cartwheels and by throwing sand in each other's eyes. Colin and Mary spread their towels side by side, stripped to their swimming suits and sat down facing the sea. A boat towing a water-skier moved across their field of vision, and some seagulls, and a boy with a tin chest strapped to his neck selling ice cream. Two of the young men were beating the arm of their friend so hard that the teenage girls cried out in protest. Immediately all the men dropped to their haunches in a horseshoe formation around the girls and introduced themselves. Colin and Mary held hands in a tight grip, working their fingers to reassure themselves that despite their silence, each was keenly aware of the other.

At breakfast Mary had repeated her story about the photograph. She did so without speculation, simply the facts in the order they had presented themselves to her. Throughout Colin nodded, mentioned that he remembered now from the night before, questioned her about one or two details (were the geranium pots in the picture? – yes; which way did the shadows fall? – she could not remember) but likewise indulged in no general remarks. He had nodded and

rubbed his eyes tiredly. Mary had gone to place her hand on
his arm and had knocked over the milk jug with her elbow.
Upstairs as they changed for the beach she had pulled him
on to the bed and hugged him hard. She had kissed his face
and cradled his head against her breasts, and told him over
and over again how she loved him, how she adored his body.
She placed her hand on his bare, tight backside and
squeezed. He nursed at her breast and sank his forefinger
deep into her. He drew his knees up, sucked and burrowed
while Mary rocked backwards and forwards, repeating his
name; then, half-crying, half-laughing she had said, 'Why is
it so frightening to love someone this hard? Why is it so
scary?' But they did not remain on the bed. They reminded
each other of their promise to go to the beach and pulled
apart to pack the towels.

Colin lay on his stomach while Mary sat astride his
buttocks and rubbed oil on his back. Eyes closed, he rested
his face sideways on the backs of his hands, and told Mary
for the first time of how Robert had hit him in the stomach.
He recounted, without embellishment or reference to his
own feelings, then or now; simply the conversation as he
could recall it, the physical positions, the exact sequence of
events. As he spoke Mary massaged his back, upwards from
the base of his spine, working the small, firm muscles with
convergent movements of her thumbs till she came to the
unyielding tendons at the back of his neck. 'That hurts,'
Colin said. Mary said, 'Go on. Finish the story.' He was
telling her now what Caroline had whispered as they were
leaving. Behind them the murmur of the young men's voices
rose steadily in volume till they erupted in general laughter,
nervous but good-natured; then the young women spoke to
each other softly and rapidly, and there was general laughter
again, less nervous, more subdued. From behind these
people came the lulling sound of waves breaking at near-
regular intervals, and waves yet more soporific when they

suggested unfathomable complexities of motion by breaking, as they occasionally did, in rapid succession. The sun blared like loud music. Colin's words slurred a little, Mary's movements were less earnest, more rhythmic. 'I heard her,' she said when Colin had finished.

'She's a kind of prisoner,' Colin said, and then, more certainly, 'She *is* a prisoner.'

'I know,' Mary said. She kept her hands in one place, looped loosely round Colin's neck, and described her conversation with Caroline on the balcony.

'Why didn't you tell me about that before?' he said at the end.

Mary hesitated. 'Why didn't you tell *me*?' She climbed off him and they sat on their own towels once more facing the sea.

After a prolonged silence Colin said, 'Perhaps he beats her up.' Mary nodded. 'And yet . . .' He lifted a handful of sand and let it trickle on to his toes. '. . . and yet she seemed to be quite . . .' He trailed away vaguely.

'Quite content?' Mary said sourly. 'Everyone knows how much women enjoy being beaten up.'

'Don't be so bloody self-righteous.' Colin's vehemence surprised them both. 'What I was going to say was that . . . she seemed to be, well, thriving on something.'

'Oh yes,' Mary said. 'Pain.'

Colin sighed and rolled back on to his stomach.

Mary pursed her lips and watched some children playing in the shallow water. 'Those postcards,' she murmured

They remained sitting for half an hour, by their slight frowns in private versions of an argument that would have been difficult to define. They were inhibited by a feeling that these past few days had been nothing more than a form of parasitism, an unacknowledged conspiracy of silence disguised by so much talk. She reached into her bag and took out a rubber band which she used to secure her hair in a pony tail. Then she stood up abruptly and walked towards the water. As she passed by the small, boisterous group, a couple of the men whistled after her softly. Mary looked back questioningly, but the men smiled sheepishly and glanced away, and one of them coughed. Colin, who had not shifted his position, watched her standing ankle-deep in water among children who laughed and screeched excitedly as they chased over the waves. Mary in her turn appeared to be watching a group of larger children, further out, who were scrambling on to and tumbling from the flat, black inner tube of a tractor tyre. She waded out till she was level with them. The children called to her, no doubt exhorting her to get in the water properly, and Mary nodded in their direction. With the briefest possible glance back over her shoulder towards Colin, she pushed forward and nestled into the water, into the comfortable, slow, breaststroke that could take her twenty effortless lengths of her local swimming-pool.

Colin lay back on his elbows, luxuriating in warmth and relative solitude. One of the men had produced a bright red beachball, and now there was a clamour about the right sort of game to be played with it, and about the more difficult question of teams. One of the girls joined in. She was stabbing her finger in mock admonition into the chest of the largest man. Her friend, who was thin and tall and a little spindly in the legs, stood apart, fiddling nervously with a strand of hair, her face fixed in a polite, acquiescent grin. She was gazing into the face of a square, ape-like figure who seemed determined to entertain her. At the end of one of his stories he reached up and gave her a friendly punch on the shoulder. A little later he darted forward and pinched her leg and ran off a few steps, turned and told her to chase him. Like a newborn calf, the girl took a few aimless steps which faltered in embarrassment. She swept her fingers through her hair and turned towards her friend. The ape came at her again and this time slapped her bottom, a skilful passing stroke, which made a surprisingly loud noise. The others, including the shorter girl, all laughed, and the ape performed an exultant, flailing cartwheel. Still smiling bravely, the spindly girl backed out of his way. Two beach-umbrella poles were planted in the sand several feet apart, joined at the top by a length of string; a game of volley-ball was about to begin. The ape, having made certain that the spindly girl was in his team, had taken her aside and was instructing her in the rules. He took hold of the ball and, showing her his bunched fist, punched it high in the air. The girl nodded and smiled. She refused her turn, but the ape persisted and she obliged by knocking the ball a few feet into the air. The ape applauded as he ran after the ball.

Colin walked by the water's edge and stooped to examine a patch of foam that had been washed ashore. In each tiny bubble the light was refracted to form a perfect rainbow in the film. The patch was drying out even as he watched it, dozens of rainbows disappearing each second, and yet none of them simultaneously. When he stood up nothing remained beyond an irregular circle of scum. Mary was now some two hundred yards from the shore, her head a small black dot against a flat grey expanse. To see her better Colin shaded his eyes. She was no longer swimming out; in fact she seemed to be facing the shore, but it was hard to make out if she was swimming towards him or treading water. As though in answer, she raised her arm and waved urgently. Was it an arm though, or a wave behind her? For a moment he lost sight of her head. It sank and reappeared, and once more there was a movement above it. Surely an arm. Colin took a sharp breath and waved back. He had taken several paces into the water without noticing. The head seemed to turn, not disappear this time, but thrash from side to side. He called Mary's name, not out loud, but in a panicky whisper. Standing in water up to his chest he took one last look at her. Once more her head disappeared, and still it was difficult to see whether she had sunk into the waves, or was concealed behind them.

He began to swim in her direction. In the same local swimming-pool, Colin performed a furious, stylish crawl that pushed a deep furrow in the water for one length, on good days two. Over great distances he was weak, and complained of the tedium of swimming up and down. Now he compromised with long strokes, breathing out with noisy sighs, as though mocking a succession of sad events. After twenty-five yards he had to stop to catch his breath. He lay on his back a few seconds, and then trod water. For all his squinting, Mary was not in sight. He set out again, this time more slowly, alternating his crawl with a sidestroke that allowed him to breathe more easily and kept his face clear of the waves which were larger now, trailing smooth troughs that were tiring to swim through. By the time he stopped again he could just make her out. He shouted, but his voice was feeble, and it seemed to weaken him to let so much air out of his lungs at once. Out there, only the top few inches of water were warm; his feet, when he trod water, were numbed by cold. As he turned to swim on, he caught a wave full in the face and swallowed a large quantity of water. It went down smoothly, but he had to turn on his back to recover. Oh God, he said, or thought, over and over again, Oh God! He started out once more, took a few strokes of the crawl and had to stop; his arms were water-logged, too heavy to lift out of the water. He used the sidestroke all the time now, edging his way through the water, making imperceptible progress. When he stopped again, spluttering for air, craning his head over the waves, Mary was ten yards away, treading water. He could not see the expression on her face. She was calling out to him, but the water slapping round his ears obscured the words. Those last few yards took a very long time. Colin's stroke had degenerated into a sideways scrambling movement, and when he had the strength to look up, Mary seemed to have moved further away. At last he reached her. He stretched his hand to her shoulder, and she sank beneath his fingers. 'Mary!' Colin shouted, and swallowed more water.

Mary reappeared, and blew her nose between her fingers. Her eyes were red and small. 'Isn't it beautiful?' she cried. Colin gasped and lunged for her shoulder again. 'Careful,' she said. 'Lie on your back or you'll drown us both.' He tried to speak, but water filled his mouth the moment it opened. 'It's so wonderful out here after those narrow streets,' Mary said.

Colin lay on his back, arms and legs spread like a starfish. His eyes were closed. 'Yes,' he said at last, with difficulty. 'It's fantastic.'

The beach was less crowded by the time they returned to it, but the volley-ball game had only just broken up. The tall girl was walking away by herself, head bowed. The other players watched as the ape bounded after, and, walking backwards in front of her, moved his arms in extravagant, imploring circles. Mary and Colin dragged their belongings under the shade of an abandoned umbrella and slept for half an hour. When they woke the beach was emptier still. The volley-ball players and their net had gone, and only those large family groups with their own picnics remained, dozing or murmuring round tables covered with debris. At Colin's suggestion they dressed and walked towards the busy avenue in search of food and drink. For once they found, in less than a quarter of an hour, a restaurant that suited them. They sat on the terrace in the thick green shade of a gnarled wisteria whose branches wound and retraced through yards of lattice-work. Their table was secluded and spread with two layers of starched pink tablecloths. The cutlery was heavy and ornate, and highly polished. In the centre of their table was a red carnation in a miniature vase of pale blue ceramic.

The two waiters who served them were friendly but pleasingly distant and the brevity of the menu suggested concentrated attention in the preparation of each dish. As it turned out, the food was unexceptional, but the wine was cool, and they drank a bottle and a half. They conversed rather than talked, politely, casually, like old acquaintances. They avoided references to themselves or to the holiday. Instead they mentioned mutual friends and wondered how they were, sketched out certain arrangements for the journey home, talked about sunburn and the relative merits of the breaststroke and crawl. Colin yawned frequently.

It was only when they were outside, walking queasily in the shade, behind them the two waiters watching from the terrace steps, ahead the straight avenue that led from the beach and open sea to the quayside and lagoon, that Colin looped his forefinger round Mary's – it was too hot to hold hands – and mentioned the photograph. Had Robert been following them around with a camera? Was he following them now? Mary shrugged and glanced back. Colin looked back too. There were cameras everywhere, suspended like aquarium fish against a watery background of limbs and clothes, but Robert, of course, was not there. 'Perhaps', Mary said, 'he thinks you have a nice face.'

Colin shrugged and, withdrawing his hand, touched his shoulders. 'I've had too much sun,' he explained.

They walked towards the quayside. The crowds were leaving the restaurants and bars now, and heading back towards the beach. To make progress Colin and Mary had to leave the pavement and walk in the road. There was only one boat at the quay when they arrived there, and it was about to leave. It was smaller than the usual boats that crossed the lagoon. Its black-painted wheel-house and funnel, which was the shape of a battered top hat, gave the boat the appearance of a dishevelled undertaker. Colin was already walking towards it, while Mary studied a schedule by the ticket office.

'It goes round the other side of the island first,' she said as she caught him up, 'then it cuts through by the harbour round to our side.'

The moment they stepped on board, the boatman went inside the wheel-house and the engine note picked up. His crew – the usual young man with moustache – cast off and slammed shut the metal barrier. For once there were very few passengers, and Colin and Mary stood several feet apart, on either side of the wheel-house, staring along the line of the prow as it swung round through distant, celebrated spires and domes, past the great clock tower till it came to rest on the cemetery island, from here no more than a hazy smear edging up over the horizon.

Now the course was set, the engine settled into a pleasant, rhythmic fluctuation between two notes that were less than a semi-tone apart. For the entire journey – some thirty-five minutes – they did not talk or even glance towards each other. They sat down on adjacent benches and continued to stare ahead. Between them stood the crew who slouched in the half-open wheel-house door and exchanged occasional remarks with the pilot. Mary rested her chin on her elbow. From time to time Colin closed his eyes.

When the boat was slowing into its approach to the landing by the hospital, he crossed to Mary's side to look at the passengers waiting to come on board, a small group, mostly old, who, despite the heat, stood as close together as possible without touching. Mary too was standing, staring towards the next stop, clearly visible over a quarter-mile of unrippled water. The elderly passengers were helped on, there was a quick exchange of shouts between the pilot and his crew, and the boat moved on, parallel to the pavement they had walked along one morning five days ago.

Colin stood close behind Mary and said in her ear, 'Perhaps we should get off at the next stop and walk through. It will be quicker than going right round the harbour.'

Mary shrugged and said, 'Perhaps.' She did not turn to look at him. But when the boat was edging towards the landing of the next stop, and the crewman was already coiling the rope round the bollard, she turned quickly and kissed him lightly on the lips. The metal barrier was lifted and a couple of passengers stepped ashore. There was a momentary pause, when everyone around them seemed poised between actions, like children at a game of grandmother's footsteps. The pilot had rested his forearm on the wheel and was looking across at his crew. He had picked up the trailing end of the rope, and was about to unwind it from the bollard. The new passengers had found their places, but the customary small-talk had yet to begin. Colin and Mary walked three paces, from the worn varnish of the deck, to the cracked, blackened boards of the landing stage, and immediately the pilot called out sharply to the crew, who nodded and lifted the rope clear. From inside the boat, the airless covered part, there came the sound of sudden laughter and several people speaking at once. Colin and Mary walked slowly and in silence along the quay. The view afforded by their occasional glances to the left was obscured by particular arrangements of trees, houses, walls, but a gap was bound to occur, and they found they had both stopped to stare past the corner of a tall electricity sub-station, between two branches of a mature plane tree, to a familiar balcony hung with flowers where a small figure in white first stared and then began to wave. Over the soft throb of that departing boat they heard Caroline calling to them. Still careful to avoid the other's eye, they walked towards an alleyway on their left which would bring them to the house. They did not hold hands.

chapter
nine

A glimpse up the stairwell, a silhouetted head, established
that Robert was waiting for them on the top landing. They
ascended in silence, Colin one or two steps ahead of Mary.
Above them they heard Robert clear his throat and speak.
Caroline was waiting there too. As they turned into the final
flight of stairs, Colin slowed and his hand sought Mary's
behind his back, but Robert had descended to meet them
and, with a resigned smile of welcome, markedly different
from his usually boisterous style, was sliding his arm round
Colin's shoulder, as though to help him up the remaining
steps, and in so doing was turning his back conspicuously on
Mary. Ahead, supporting herself awkwardly in the doorway
of the apartment, wearing a white dress with square, efficient
pockets, stood Caroline, her smile a horizontal line of quiet
satisfaction. Their greetings were intimate yet restrained,
decorous; Colin was steered towards Caroline who offered
him her cheek and at the same time held his hand lightly for
an instant. All the while, Robert, dressed in a dark suit with
waistcoat, white shirt, but no tie, black boots with high
tapering heels, kept his hand on Colin's shoulder, releasing
him only to turn at last to Mary towards whom he made the
faintest of ironic bows and whose hand he held till she
withdrew it, stepped round him and exchanged kisses, barely
a grazing of cheeks, with Caroline. Now they were bunched
closely by the door, but there was no move to go inside.

'The boat brought us round this side from the beach,' Mary explained, 'so we thought we'd say hello.'

'We were expecting you sooner,' Robert said. He rested his hand on Mary's arm and spoke to her as though they were alone. 'Colin made a promise to my wife which he seems to have forgotten. I left a message at your hotel this morning.'

Caroline too addressed herself solely to Mary. 'We're going away too, you see. We were anxious not to miss you.'

'Why?' Colin said suddenly.

Robert and Caroline smiled, and Mary, covering for this small indiscretion, asked politely, 'Where are you going?'

Caroline looked at Robert who took a pace backward from the group and rested his hand on the wall. 'Oh, a long journey. Caroline has not seen her parents for many years. But we'll tell you about that.' He took a handkerchief from his pocket and dabbed at his brow. 'First there is a little business I must conclude at my bar.' He spoke to Caroline. 'Take Mary indoors and give her some refreshments. Colin will come with me.' Caroline retreated a couple of steps into the apartment and gestured at Mary to follow her.

Mary in her turn reached for the beach bag from Colin and was about to speak to him when Robert placed himself between them. 'Go inside,' he said. 'We will not be very long.'

Colin too was starting to speak to Mary, and craning his neck to catch a sight of her round Robert, but the door was closing and Robert was steering him gently towards the stairs.

It was customary here for men to walk in public hand in hand, or arm in arm; Robert held Colin's hand tightly, the fingers interlocking and exerting a constant pressure such that to have withdrawn would have required a wilful movement, possibly insulting, certainly eccentric. They were taking yet another unfamiliar route, along streets relatively free of tourists and souvenir shops, a quarter from which women too seemed to have been excluded, for everywhere, in the frequent bars and street cafés, at strategic street-corners or canal bridges, in the one or two pinball arcades they passed, were men of all ages, mostly in shirtsleeves, chatting in small groups, though here and there individuals dozed with newspapers on their laps. Small boys stood on the peripheries, their arms folded importantly like their fathers and brothers.

Everyone seemed to know Robert, and he appeared to be choosing a route which would include the maximum of encounters, leading Colin across a canal for a quick conversation outside a bar, doubling back to a small square where a group of older men stood round a disused fountain whose bowl overflowed with crumpled cigarette packets. Colin was not able to follow the conversations, though the sound of his own name seemed to recur. As they were turning to leave one boisterous group outside a pinball arcade, someone pinched his buttock hard and he turned angrily. But Robert pulled him on and loud laughter followed them to the end of the street.

Despite the new manager, a broad-shouldered man with tattooed forearms who rose to greet them as they came in, Robert's bar was unchanged; the same blue glow from the juke-box, now silent, the line of black-legged bar stools topped in red plastic, the invariably static quality of an artificially-lit basement room untouched by the cycle of day and night outside. It was barely four o'clock and there were no more than half a dozen customers, all standing at the bar. What was new, or more apparent, was the number of large black flies which cruised silently between the tables like predatory fish. Colin shook the manager's hand, asked for a glass of mineral water and sat down at the table they had sat at before.

Having excused himself, Robert went behind the bar with the manager to examine some papers that were spread out on the counter. The two men appeared to be signing an agreement. An iced bottle of mineral water, a glass and bowl of pistachio nuts were set down in front of Colin by a bar-hand. Seeing Robert straighten from the papers and look in his direction, Colin raised his glass in acknowledgment, but Robert, though he continued to stare, did not alter his expression, and, nodding slowly at some thought of his own, lowered his gaze once more to the documents before him. One by one the few drinkers at the bar also turned to glance at Colin, and then back to their drinks and conversation. Colin sipped his drink, prised open the nuts and ate them, put his hands in his pockets, tilted his chair back on two legs. When another of the customers looked at Colin over his shoulder and then turned to his neighbour who in turn shifted position to catch his eye, Colin stood up and walked purposefully towards the juke-box.

He stood with folded arms and gazed at the banks of unfamiliar names and incomprehensible titles, as though stuck for a choice. The drinkers at the bar now watched him with undisguised curiosity. He dropped a coin into the machine. The configuration of illuminated signs altered drastically, and a rectangle of red light began to pulse, urging him to choose. From behind him by the bar someone spoke loudly a short phrase which could easily have been the title of a song. Colin searched the columns of typewritten tabs, passing and immediately returning to the name of a record which alone among the names had meaning – 'Ha ha ha' – and even as he punched out the numbers and the great device vibrated beneath his fingers, he knew it was the virile, sentimental song they had heard last time. As Colin made his way back to his seat, Robert's manager lifted his head and smiled. The customers called for the volume to be increased and when the first deafening chorus burst across the room, a fresh round of drinks was ordered by a man who slapped the counter in time to the strict, almost martial, rhythm.

Robert came to sit by Colin and studied his documents while the record reached its climax. When the machine clicked off, he smiled broadly and pointed at the empty mineral-water bottle. Colin shook his head. Robert offered a cigarette and, frowning at Colin's emphatic refusal, lit one for himself and said: 'Did you understand what I was telling people as we walked here?' Colin shook his head. 'Not one single word?'

'No.'

Robert smiled again in simple delight. 'Everyone we met, I told them that you are my lover, that Caroline is very jealous, and that we are coming here to drink and forget about her.'

Colin was tucking his T-shirt into his jeans. He ran his fingers through his hair and looked up, blinking. 'Why?'

Robert laughed and mimicked accurately Colin's studious hesitancy. 'Why? Why?' Then he leaned forwards and touched Colin's forearm. 'We knew you would come back. We were waiting, preparing. We thought you'd come sooner.'

'Preparing?' Colin said, withdrawing his arm. Robert folded the papers into his pocket and gazed at him with proprietorial tenderness.

Colin was about to speak, hesitated, and then said quickly, 'Why did you take that picture of me?'

Robert was all smiles once more. He leaned back, one arm slung over the back of his chair, beaming self-satisfaction. 'I thought I did not give her enough time. Mary is very quick.'

'What's the point,' Colin insisted, but a newcomer to the bar had crossed to the juke-box and 'Ha ha ha' was starting again at even greater volume. Colin folded his arms and Robert stood to greet a group of friends who were passing their table.

On the walk home, this time by the less crowded, descending street that took them, for part of their way, along the seafront, Colin pressed Robert about the photograph again, and what he had meant by preparations, but Robert was buoyantly evasive, pointing out, in reply, the barber shop used by his grandfather, his father and himself, explaining, with an intensity and long-windedness that may have been parodic, how pollution from the city affected the livelihoods of fishermen, and forced them to take jobs as waiters. Mildly exasperated, Colin stopped suddenly but Robert, though he slowed his energetic stride and turned in surprise, sauntered on as though it was a matter of pride with him not to stop too.

Colin was close to the spot where he had sat with Mary on packing cases and watched the early morning sun. Now, in the late afternoon, although the sun was still high, the eastern sky had lost its vivid purple and, fading by degrees through nursery blue to diluted milk, effected, across the precise line of the horizon, the most delicate of transactions with the pale grey of the sea. The island cemetery, its low stone wall, the packed, bright headstones, was picked out clearly by the sun at his back. Colin glanced across his left shoulder along the quay. Robert was fifty yards away, walking unhurriedly towards him. Colin turned round to look behind. A narrow commercial street, barely more than an alley, broke the line of weatherbeaten houses. It wound under shop awnings and under washing hung like bunting from tiny wrought-iron balconies, and vanished enticingly into shadow. It asked to be explored, but explored alone, without consultations with, or obligations towards, a companion. To step down there now as if completely free, to be released from the arduous states of play of psychological condition, to have leisure to be open and attentive to perception, to the world whose breathtaking, incessant cascade against the senses was so easily and habitually ignored, dinned out, in the interests of unexamined ideals of personal responsibility, efficiency, citizenship, to step down there now, just walk away, melt into the shadow, would be so very easy.

Robert cleared his throat softly. He was standing a couple of paces to Colin's left. Colin turned back to look at the sea again and said lightly, companionably, 'The thing about a successful holiday is that it makes you want to go home.'

It was a full minute before Robert spoke, and when he did there was a trace of regret in his voice. 'It's time to go,' he said.

The gallery, as Mary stepped inside and Caroline closed the door firmly behind her, appeared to have doubled in size. Practically all the furniture, and all the pictures, rugs, chandeliers and wall hangings had vanished. Where the great, polished table had stood were three boxes supporting a thick plywood board on which were spread the remains of a lunch. Around this makeshift table were four chairs. The floor was an open plain of marble, and Mary's sandals flopped and echoed loudly as she advanced a few paces into the room. All that remained of significance was Robert's sideboard, his shrine. Behind Mary, just inside the door, were two suitcases. The balcony was still profuse with plants, but the furniture had gone from there too.

Caroline, who was still standing by the door, smoothed her dress with the palms of her hands. 'I don't usually dress like a ward sister,' she said, 'but with so many things to arrange, I feel more efficient in white.'

Mary smiled. 'I'm inefficient in any colour.'

Out of context, it might have been difficult to recognize Caroline. The hair, so tightly drawn back before, was slightly awry; loose strands softened her face which in the intervening days had lost its anonymity. The lips especially, previously so thin and bloodless, were full, almost sensual. The long straight line of her nose, where formerly it had appeared no more than the least acceptable solution to a problem of design, now conferred dignity. The eyes had shed their hard, mad shine and seemed more communicative, sympathetic. Only her skin remained unchanged, without colour, without even pallor, a toneless grey.

'You look well,' Mary said.

Caroline came forward, the same painful, awkward gait, and took Mary's hands in hers. 'I'm glad you came,' she said, urgently hospitable, squeezing tight on 'glad' and 'came'. 'We knew Colin would keep his promise.'

She went to withdraw her hands but Mary kept hold. 'We didn't exactly plan to come, but it wasn't completely accidental either. I wanted to talk to you.' Caroline sustained her smile, but her hands were heavy in Mary's, who still would not let go. She nodded as Mary spoke and directed her gaze at the floor. 'I've been wondering about you. There are some things I wanted to ask you.'

'Ah well,' Caroline said after a pause, 'let's go in the kitchen. I'll make some herb tea.' She pulled her hands free, this time a decisive tug, and, resuming the intent manner of the serious hostess, beamed at Mary before she turned briskly and limped away.

The kitchen was at the same end of the gallery as the entrance to the apartment. It was small, but immaculately neat, with many cupboards and drawers, and surfaces coated in white plastic. The lighting was fluorescent, and there was no sign of food. From a cupboard under the sink Caroline produced a stool of tubular steel and gave it to Mary to sit on. The cooker was supported by a worn card table and was of the kind found in caravans, with two rings, no oven, and a length of rubber hose which ran into a gas

bottle on the floor. Caroline put a kettle on to boil and
reached, with great difficulty and a curt refusal of help, into
a cupboard for a teapot. She stood still for a moment, one
hand resting on the refrigerator, the other on her hip, and
appeared to be waiting for a pain to pass. Immediately
behind her was another door, slightly ajar, through which
Mary could see the corner of a bed.

When Caroline had recovered and was spooning small,
dried flowers from a jar into the teapot, Mary said lightly,
'What did you do to your back?'

Once again there flashed the ready smile, hardly more
than a baring of teeth and a rapid forward movement of the
jaw, the kind of smile offered to mirrors, all the stranger here
in this confined, bright space. 'It's been like this a long time
now,' she said, and busied herself with cups and saucers. She
began to tell Mary of her travel plans; she and Robert were
flying to Canada and there they would stay with her parents
for three months. When they returned they would buy
another house, a ground-floor apartment, perhaps,
somewhere with no stairs. She had filled two cups and was
slicing a lemon.

Mary agreed that the journey sounded exciting and the
plan sensible. 'But what about the pain,' she said. 'Is it your
spine, or your hip? Have you seen anyone about it?' Caroline
had turned her back on Mary and was putting the lemon
slices into the tea. At the clink of a teaspoon Mary added,
'No sugar for me.'

Caroline turned and gave her her cup. 'Just stirring in the
lemon,' she said, 'to make it taste.' They carried their cups
out of the kitchen. 'I'll tell you about my back,' Caroline
said as she led the way on to the balcony, 'when you've told
me how good you think this tea is. Orange blossom.'

Mary rested her cup on the balcony wall and fetched two
chairs from indoors. They sat as before, though less
comfortably and without a table between them, facing out to

sea and the nearby island. Because these chairs were higher, Mary had a view of that part of the quay from which she and Colin had caught sight of Caroline, who was now raising her cup as though to propose a toast. Mary swallowed, and though its tartness caused her to purse her lips, she said it was refreshing. They drank in silence, Mary watching Caroline steadily, expectantly, and Caroline glancing up from her lap every so often to smile nervously at Mary. When both cups were empty Caroline began abruptly.

'Robert said he told you about his childhood. He exaggerates a lot, and turns his past into stories to tell at the bar, but all the same it was weird. My childhood was happy and dull. I was an only child, and my father, who was very kind, doted on me, and I did everything he said. I was very close to my mother, we were almost like sisters, and between us we worked hard looking after Dad, "backing up the ambassador" my mother used to say. I was twenty when I married Robert and I knew nothing about sex. Until that time, as far as I can remember, I hadn't had any sexual feelings at all. Robert had been about a bit, so after a bad start it began to come alive for me. Everything was fine. I was trying to get pregnant. Robert was desperate to be a father, desperate to have sons, but nothing came of it. For a long time the doctors thought it was me, but in the end it turned out to be Robert, something wrong with his sperm. He's very sensitive about it. The doctors said we should keep on trying. But then, something started to happen. You're the first person I've told. I can't even remember the first time now, or what we thought was going on at the time. We must have talked about it, but just possibly we didn't. I can't remember. Robert started to hurt me when we made love. Not a lot, but enough to make me cry out. I think I tried hard to stop him. One night I got really angry at him, but he went on doing it, and I had to admit, though it took a long time, that I liked it. Perhaps you find that hard to understand. It's not the pain itself, it's the fact of the pain, of being helpless before it and being reduced to nothing by it. It's pain in a particular context, being punished and therefore being guilty. We both liked what was happening. I was ashamed of myself, and before I knew it, my shame too was a source of pleasure. It was as if I was discovering something that had been with me all my life. I wanted it more and more. I needed it. Robert began to really hurt me. He used a whip. He beat me with his fists as he made love to me. I was terrified, but the terror and the pleasure were all one. Instead of saying loving things into my ear, he whispered pure hatred, and though I was sick with humiliation, I thrilled to the point of passing out. I didn't doubt Robert's hatred for me. It wasn't theatre. He made love to me out of deep loathing, and I couldn't resist. I loved being punished.

'We went on like this for some time. My body was covered in bruises, cuts, weals. Three of my ribs were cracked. Robert knocked out one of my teeth. I had a broken finger. I didn't dare visit my parents and as soon as Robert's grandfather died we moved here. To Robert's friends I was just another beaten wife, which was exactly what I was. Nobody noticed. It gave Robert some status round the places where he drank. When I was alone for long enough, or when I was out with ordinary people doing ordinary things, the madness of what we were doing, and my own acquiescence in it, terrified me. I kept telling myself I had to get away. And then, as soon as we were back together again, what had seemed mad became inevitable, even logical, once more. Neither of us could resist it. Quite often I was the one to initiate it, and that was never difficult. Robert was longing to pound my body to a pulp. We had arrived at the point we had been heading towards all the time. Robert confessed one night that there was only one thing he really wanted. He wanted to kill me, as we made love. He was absolutely serious. I remember the next day we went to a restaurant and tried to laugh it off. But the idea kept coming back. Because of that possibility hanging over us, we made love like never before.

'One night Robert came in from an evening of drinking, just as I was falling asleep. He got into bed and took me from behind. He whispered he was going to kill me, but he'd said that many times before. He had his forearm round my neck, and then he began to push into the small of my back. At the same time he pulled my head backwards. I blacked out with the pain, but even before I went I remember thinking: it's going to happen. I can't go back on it now. Of course, I wanted to be destroyed.

'My back was broken and I was in hospital for months. I'll never walk properly now, partly because of an incompetent surgeon, although the other specialists say he did a wonderful job. They cover for each other. I can't bend down, I get pains in my legs and in my hip joint. It's very difficult for me to walk down stairs, and completely impossible to walk up them. Ironically, the only position I'm comfortable in is on my back. By the time I came out of the hospital, Robert had bought the bar with his grandfather's money, and it was a success. This week he's selling it to the manager. When I came out, the idea was that we were going to be sensible. We were shaken up by what had happened. Robert was putting all his energy into the bar, I was seeing a physiotherapist here in the apartment several hours a day. But of course, we couldn't forget what we'd been through, nor could we stop wanting it. We were the same people after all, and this idea, I mean the idea of death, wouldn't go away just because we said it had to. We didn't talk about it, it was impossible to talk about it, but it showed through in different ways. When the physiotherapist said I was strong enough, I went out by myself, just to walk in the streets and be an ordinary person again. When I came home I discovered that I couldn't get up the stairs. If I put all my weight on one leg and pushed, I felt a terrible pain, like an electric shock. I waited out in the courtyard for Robert to come home. When he did, he said it was my own fault for leaving the apartment without his permission. He spoke to me like a small child. He wouldn't help me up the stairs, and he wouldn't let any of the neighbours come near me either. You'll find this hard to believe, but I had to stay out all night. I sat in a doorway and tried to sleep, and all night I thought I heard people snoring in their bedrooms. In the morning Robert carried me up the stairs and we had our first sex since I had been out of the hospital.

'I became a virtual prisoner. I could leave the apartment any time, but I could never be sure of getting back, and in the end I gave up. Robert has been paying a neighbour to do all our shopping, and I've hardly been outside in four years. I looked after the heirlooms, Robert's little museum. He's obsessed with his father and grandfather. And I made this garden out here. I've spent a lot of time by myself. It hasn't been so bad.' Caroline broke off and looked sharply at Mary. 'Have you understood what I've been talking about?' Mary nodded, and Caroline softened. 'Good. It's very important to me that you understand exactly what I've been saying.' She was fingering the large, glossy leaves of a potted plant on the balcony wall. She pulled away a dead leaf and let it drop into the courtyard below. 'Now,' she announced, but did not finish her sentence.

The sun had disappeared behind the roof at their back. Mary shivered and stifled a yawn. 'I haven't bored you,' Caroline said. It was more a statement than a question.

Mary said she was not bored, and explained how the long

swim, the sleep in the sun and the heavy restaurant meal had made her feel drowsy. Then, because Caroline was still looking at her intently, expectantly, she added, 'What now? Will going home help you become more independent?'

Caroline shook her head. 'We'll tell you about that when Robert and Colin are here.' She set about asking Mary a series of questions about Colin, some of which she had asked before. Were Mary's children fond of him? Did he take a special interest in them? Did Colin know her ex-husband? Throughout Mary's brief and polite replies, Caroline nodded, as though checking off items on a list.

When, quite unexpectedly, she asked if she and Colin had done 'strange things' Mary smiled good-humouredly at her. 'Sorry. We're very ordinary people. You'll have to take that on trust.' Caroline became silent, her eyes were fixed on the ground. Mary leaned forward to touch her hand. 'I didn't mean to be rude. I don't know you that well. You had something to tell, so you told it, which was good. I didn't force it out of you.' Mary's hand lay on Caroline's several seconds, squeezing gently.

Caroline had closed her eyes. Then she grasped Mary's hand and stood as quickly as she was able. 'There's something I want to show you,' she said through the effort of rising.

Mary stood too, partly in order to help her up. 'Isn't that Colin way over there,' she said, and indicated a solitary figure on the quay, just visible beyond the topmost branches of a tree.

Caroline looked and shrugged. I'd need my glasses to see that far.' Still holding Mary's hand, she was already turning towards the door.

They went through the kitchen into the bedroom which was in semi-darkness for the shutters were closed. For all Caroline's account of what had happened there, it was a

bare, unexceptional room. As in the guest room at the other
end of the gallery, a louvred door gave on to a tiled
bathroom. The bed was large, without headboard or pillows,
and was covered by a pale green bedspread, smooth to the
touch.

Mary sat down on the edge of the bed. 'My legs ache,' she
said, more to herself than to Caroline who was pulling the
shutters open. The room was flooded with late afternoon
light, and Mary was suddenly aware that the wall adjacent
to the window, the wall behind her which ran the length of
the bed, supported a wide baize-covered board covered with
numerous photographs, overlapping like a collage, mostly
black and white, a few Polaroids in colour, all of them of
Colin. Mary moved along the bed to see more clearly, and
Caroline came and sat close beside her.

'He's very beautiful,' she said softly. 'Robert saw you
both, quite by chance, the day you first arrived.' She pointed
at a picture of Colin standing by a suitcase, a street map in
his hand. He was talking over his shoulder to someone,
perhaps Mary, just out of frame. 'We both think he's very
beautiful.' Caroline placed her arm round Mary's shoulders.
'Robert took a lot of pictures that day, but that's the one I
saw first. I'll never forget it. Just looking up from the map.
Robert came home so excited. Then as he brought more
pictures home' – Caroline indicated the whole board – 'we
became closer and closer again. It was my idea to put them
up here, where we could see them all at once. We would lie
here into the early morning making plans. You'd never
believe how much planning there was to do.'

While Caroline talked, Mary rubbed her legs, sometimes
massaging, sometimes scratching, and studied the mosaic of
the past week. There were pictures whose context she
understood immediately. Several showed Colin on the
balcony more clearly than the grainy print. There were

pictures of Colin walking into the hotel, another of him sitting alone on the café pontoon, of Colin standing in a crowd, pigeons at his feet, the great clock tower in the background. In one he lay naked on a bed. Other pictures were less easily understood. One taken at night, in very poor light, showed Colin and Mary crossing a deserted square. In the foreground was a dog. In some photographs Colin was quite alone, in many the composition of the enlargement cut Mary off at the hand or elbow, or left a meaningless portion of face. Together the pictures seemed to have frozen every familiar expression, the puzzled frown, the puckered lips about to speak, the eyes so readily softened by endearments, and each picture held, and appeared to celebrate, a different aspect of that fragile face – the eyebrows that met at a point, the deep-set eyes, the long, straight mouth just parted by the glint of a tooth. 'Why?' Mary said at last. Her tongue was thick and heavy, and lay across the path of the word. 'Why?' she repeated with more determination, but the word, because she suddenly understood the answer, left her as a whisper. Caroline hugged Mary tighter to her and went on. 'Then Robert brought you home. It was as if God was in on our plan. I came into the bedroom. I never concealed that from you. I knew then that fantasy was passing into reality. Have you ever experienced that? It's like stepping into a mirror.'

Mary's eyes were closing. Caroline's voice was receding from her. She forced her eyes open and attempted to stand, but Caroline's arm was tight around her. Her eyes closed once more and she mouthed Colin's name. Her tongue was too heavy to lift round the 'l', it needed several people to help move it, people whose own names did not have an 'l'. Caroline's words were all about her, heavy, meaningless, tumbling objects which numbed Mary's legs. Then Caroline was slapping her face and she was waking as though into another time in history. 'You've been asleep,' she was saying, 'you've been asleep. You've been asleep. Robert and Colin are back. They'll be waiting for us. Come on now.' She pulled her into a standing position, draped Mary's helpless arm over her shoulder, and walked her out of the room.

chapter

ten

With the three windows wide open, the gallery was incandescent with afternoon sunlight. Robert stood with his back to a window, patiently removing the little wire cage from the neck of the champagne bottle in his hand. At his feet was the crumpled gold foil and at his side was Colin, two glasses at the ready, still taking in the cavernous emptiness of the room. Both men turned and nodded as the two women entered from the kitchen. Mary had steadied herself and was now walking in short, fumbling steps, one hand resting on Caroline's shoulder.

The painful limp, the somnambulant shuffle, they were making slow progress towards the makeshift table as Colin took a couple of paces in their direction and called, 'What is it, Mary?' Immediately the cork popped and Robert called sharply for the glasses. Colin retreated and held them out while watching anxiously over his shoulder. Caroline was settling Mary in one of the two remaining wooden chairs, arranging it so that she sat facing the men.

Mary parted her lips and gazed at Colin. He was walking towards her, full glass in hand, as though in slow motion. The bright light behind him fired loose strands of hair and his face, more familiar than her own, was concentrated in concern. Robert set down the bottle on his sideboard, and followed Colin across the room. Caroline stood erect by

Mary's chair, like an attendant nurse. 'Mary,' Colin said, 'what is the matter?'

They crowded round. Caroline pressed her palm against Mary's forehead. 'It's a mild touch of sunstroke,' she said quietly. 'Nothing to worry about. She said you went for a long swim and lay in the sun.'

Mary's lips moved. Colin took her hand. 'She's not hot,' he said. Robert moved behind the chair and put his arm round Caroline's shoulders. Colin squeezed Mary's hand and searched her face. Her eyes, wide with longing, or desperation, were fixed on his own; a tear welled suddenly and dropped on to the ridge of her cheekbone. Colin wiped it with his forefinger. 'Are you ill?' he whispered. 'Is it sunstroke?' She closed her eyes for a moment, and her head moved just once from side to side. The faintest sound, barely more than a breath, left her lips. Colin leaned close and put his ear to her mouth. 'Tell me,' he urged, 'try and tell me.' She drew breath sharply, and held it for several seconds, then articulated from the back of her throat a strangled, hard C. 'Are you saying my name?' Mary opened her mouth wider, she was breathing quickly, almost panting. She held Colin's hand in a ferocious grip. Again, the sharp intake of air, the breath held, and again the distant hard C. She repeated it softened, ch ... ch. Colin pressed his ear closer to her lips. Robert too was leaning over. With another immense effort she managed 'G ... G', and then whispered, 'Go.'

'Cold,' said Robert. 'She's cold.'

Caroline pushed firmly at Colin's shoulder, 'We shouldn't crowd round. It doesn't make it easier for her.'

Robert had fetched his white jacket and was draping it round Mary's shoulders. She still held Colin's hand tightly, her face was tilted up towards his, and her eyes searched his face for understanding. 'She wants to go,' Colin said desperately. 'She needs a doctor.' He wrenched his hand free of Mary's grip, and patted her wrist. She watched him wander aimlessly up the gallery. 'Where's your telephone. Surely you've got a telephone.' There was panic in his voice. Robert and Caroline, still keeping close, were following him, blocking her view of him. She tried once more to make a sound; her throat was soft and useless, her tongue an immovable weight on the floor of her mouth.

'We're going away,' Caroline said, soothingly. 'The phone has been disconnected.'

Colin had circled round to the middle window and now he stood with his back to Robert's sideboard. 'Go and fetch a doctor then. She's very ill.'

'There's no need to shout,' Robert said quietly. He and Caroline were still walking towards Colin. Mary could see how they held hands, how tightly their fingers were interlocked, and how their fingers caressed in quick, pulsing movements.

'Mary will be fine,' Caroline said. 'She had something special in her tea, but she'll be fine.'

'Tea?' Colin echoed dully. As he backed off at their approach, he nudged the table and upset the champagne bottle.

'What a waste,' Robert said, as Colin turned quickly and righted it. Robert and Caroline stepped round the puddle on the floor, and Robert stretched out his arm towards Colin, as though he were about to take his chin between finger and thumb. Colin lifted his head back and retreated another step. Directly behind him was the large open window. Mary could see how the western sky was softening, and how traces of high cloud were arranging themselves into long, fine fingers that seemed to point to where the sun must set.

The couple had separated now and were pressing in either side of Colin. He was looking straight at Mary, and all she could do now was part her lips. Caroline had placed her hand on Colin's chest and was stroking him as she spoke.

'Mary understands. I've explained everything to her. Secretly, I think you understand too.' She began to pull his T-shirt free of his jeans. Robert leaned his outstretched arm against the wall at the level of Colin's head, boxing him in. Caroline was caressing his belly, gently pinching the skin between her fingers. And though Mary was watching into the light, and the three figures by the window were silhouetted by the sky behind, she saw with total clarity the obscene precision of every movement, of every nuance of a private fantasy. The intensity of her vision had drained her faculties of speech and movement. Robert's free hand was exploring Colin's face, probing his lips apart with his fingers, tracing the lines of his nose and jaw. For a full minute he stood still and unresisting, paralysed by sheer incomprehension. Only his face changed through wonderment and fear, narrowing to puzzlement and the effort of memory. His eyes remained fixed on hers.

The usual end-of-day clamour rose from the packed streets below – voices, kitchen chatter, television sets – intensifying rather than filling the silence in the gallery. Colin's body began to tense. Mary could see the trembling in his legs, the tightening across the stomach. Caroline made a shushing noise, and her hand came to rest just under his heart. At that moment Colin sprang forward, his arms before him like a diver, banging Caroline's face out of his path with his forearm, catching Robert on the shoulder, a blow that pushed him back a step. Colin came towards Mary through the gap between them, his arms still outstretched, as though he might scoop her from her chair, and fly to safety with her. Robert had recovered in time to dart forward and catch hold of Colin's ankle, and tip him to the floor, a few feet from Mary's chair. He was already scrambling to stand when Robert picked him up by an arm and a leg, and half-carried, half-dragged him back to where Caroline stood nursing her face. There he stood Colin on his feet and slammed him hard against the wall, and held him there, his enormous hand firm round Colin's throat.

Now the trio had reassembled before Mary in approximately their former positions. The rasp of heavy breathing gradually subsided, and once more the neighbourly sounds were audible, framing the silence in the room.

At last Robert said quietly, 'That was completely unnecessary, wasn't it?' He tightened his grip. 'Wasn't it?' Colin nodded, and Robert removed his hand.

'Look,' Caroline said, 'you've cut my lip.' She collected blood from her lower lip on to her forefinger and daubed it on Colin's lips. He did not resist her. Robert's hand still rested at the base of his neck close to his throat. Caroline transferred more of her blood on the end of her finger till Colin's lips were completely and accurately rouged. Then Robert, pressing his forearm against the top of Colin's chest, kissed him deeply on the mouth, and as he did so, Caroline ran her hand over Robert's back.

When he straightened, Colin spat loudly several times. Caroline wiped the pinkish streaks of saliva from his chin with the back of her hand. 'Silly boy,' she whispered.

'What have you given Mary?' Colin said levelly. 'What do you want?'

'Want?' Robert said. He had taken something from his sideboard, but he kept his hand round it, and Mary could not see what it was. 'Want isn't a very good word.'

Caroline laughed delightedly. 'Nor is need.' She stepped back from Colin and looked over her shoulder at Mary. 'Still awake?' she called. 'Do you remember everything I've told you?'

Mary was watching the object Robert clasped in his hand. Suddenly it was twice its length, and she saw it clearly, and though every muscle in her body tightened, only the fingers of her right hand clenched softly. She shouted, and shouted again, and all that left her was a whispering exhalation.

'I'll do whatever you want,' Colin said, the level tone all lost now at that sound, his voice rising in panic. 'But please get a doctor for Mary.'

'Very well,' Robert said and reached for Colin's arm, and turned his palm upward. 'See how easy it is,' he said, perhaps to himself, as he drew the razor lightly, almost playfully, across Colin's wrist, opening wide the artery. His arm jerked forward, and the rope he cast, orange in this light, fell short of Mary's lap by several inches.

Mary's eyes closed. When she opened them, Colin was sitting on the floor, against the wall, his legs splayed before him. Curiously, his canvas beach-shoes were soaked, stained scarlet. His head swayed upon his shoulders, but his eyes were steady and pure, and blazed at her across the room in disbelief. 'Mary?' he said anxiously, like someone calling in a dark room. 'Mary? Mary?'

'I'm coming,' Mary said. 'I'm over here.'

When she woke again, after an interminable sleep, his head reclined against the wall, and his body had shrunk. His eyes, still open, still on her, were tired, without expression. She saw him from a great distance, though her vision excluded all else, sitting before a small pond that reddened with the barred rhomboid of light cast by the shutters, now half-closed.

All through the night that followed she dreamed of moans and whimpers, and sudden shouts, of figures locked and turning at her feet, churning through the little pond, calling out for joy. She was woken by the sun rising over the balcony behind her, warming her neck through the plate-glass doors. A long, long time had passed, for the many tracks across the floor were rusty, and the luggage by the door had gone.

*

Before ascending the gravel driveway to the hospital, Mary paused to rest in the shadow of the gatehouse. The weary young official at her side was patient. He set down his briefcase, took off his sunglasses and polished them with a handkerchief from his breast pocket. The women were setting up their stalls, ready for the first morning visitors. A battered van with corrugated tin sides was delivering flowers to the vendors and, nearer, a woman was taking crosses, statuettes and prayer books from an airline holdall and setting them out on a folding table. In the distance, in front of the hospital doors, a gardener was watering the drive, keeping down the dust. The official cleared his throat quietly. Mary nodded, and they set off once more.

It had become apparent that the packed, chaotic city concealed a thriving, intricate bureaucracy, a hidden order of governmental departments with separate but overlapping functions, distinct procedures and hierarchies; unpretentious doors, in streets she had passed down many times before, led not to private homes but to empty waiting-rooms with railway-station clocks, and the sound of incessant typing, and to cramped offices with brown linoleum floors. She was questioned, cross-questioned, photographed; she dictated statements, initialled documents, and stared at pictures. She carried a sealed envelope from one department to another and was questioned again. The tired, youngish men in blazers – policemen perhaps, or civil servants – treated her with courtesy, as did their superiors. Once her marital status had been clarified, and the fact that her children were several hundred miles away, and especially once she had insisted in response to repeated questions, that it had never been her intention to marry Colin, she was treated with courtesy and suspicion. She became more clearly a source of information and less an object for their concern.

But pity would have broken her. As it was, her state of

shock was prolonged, her feelings were simply unavailable to her. She did exactly as she was told without complaint and answered every question. Her lack of affect augmented the suspicion. In the assistant commissioner's office she was complimented on the precision and logical consistency of her statement, on its avoidance of distorting emotion. The official said coolly, 'Not like a woman's statement at all', and there were quiet chuckles behind her. While they clearly did not believe she had committed any crime, she was treated as though tainted by what the assistant commissioner himself had called, and had translated for her benefit, 'these obscene excesses'. Behind their questions was an assumption – or was this her imagination? – that she was the kind of person they could reasonably expect to be present at such a crime, like an arsonist at someone else's blaze.

At the same time, they were courteous enough to describe the crime back to her as wearyingly common, belonging in a well-established category. This particular department had dealt with several such crimes, differing in details of course, in the past ten years. A senior uniformed policeman who brought Mary a cup of coffee in the waiting-room sat down close beside her and explained some of the key characteristics. For example, the victim publicly displayed by the assailant, and clearly identified with him. And then, the ambivalence of the preparations; on the one hand thorough – he counted on fat fingers the photography, acquisition of the drug, selling up the contents of the apartment, packing the suitcases well in advance; on the other hand, wilfully clumsy – again he ticked them off – like leaving the razor behind, booking flights, travelling on legitimate passports.

The policeman's list was longer, but Mary had ceased to listen. He concluded by tapping her knee and saying that for these people it was as if being caught and punished was as important as the crime itself. Mary shrugged. The words 'victim', 'assailant', 'the crime itself' meant nothing, corresponded to nothing at all.

In the hotel room she folded and packed the clothes into their separate bags. Because he had a little more space, she tucked her shoes and a cotton jacket among Colin's things, just as she had for the journey out. She gave the loose change to the maid, and put the postcards between the last pages of her passport. She crumbled the remaining marihuana, and washed it down the hand basin. In the evening she spoke to the children on the phone. They were friendly but remote, and asked her several times to repeat herself. She could hear a television at their end, and at hers she heard her own voice through the receiver, wheedling for affection. Her ex-husband came on the line and said he was making a curry. She was coming to collect the children on Thursday afternoon? Couldn't she be more precise? After the phone call she sat on the edge of her bed a long time reading the small print in her plane ticket. From outside she heard the steady chipping of steel tools.

At the hospital doors the uniformed guard nodded curtly over her head to the official. They descended two flights of stairs and walked along a cool, deserted corridor. Attached to the walls at regular intervals were red drums of hosepipe and, beneath them, buckets of sand. They stopped at a door with a circular window. The official asked her to wait, and went in. Half a minute later he opened the door for her. In his hand he held a sheaf of papers. The room was small, windowless and heavily perfumed. It was lit by a fluorescent strip. Double swing-doors, also with circular windows, gave on to a larger room in which twin banks of hooded strip-lighting were visible. The narrow high bench which supported Colin protruded across the room. By it was a wooden stool. Colin lay on his back covered by a sheet. The official removed it deftly and glanced towards her; the formal identification, in the presence of the body and the official, was made. Mary signed, the official signed, and discreetly withdrew.

After a while Mary sat on the stool and put her hand in Colin's. She was in the mood for explanation, she was going to speak to Colin. She was going to recount Caroline's story, as closely as she could remember it, and then she was going to explain it all to him, tell him her theory, tentative at this stage, of course, which explained how the imagination, the sexual imagination, men's ancient dreams of hurting, and women's of being hurt, embodied and declared a powerful single organizing principle, which distorted all relations, all truth. But she explained nothing, for a stranger had arranged Colin's hair the wrong way. She combed it with her fingers and said nothing at all. She held his hand and worried his fingers. She mouthed his name several times without uttering it, as if repetition could have returned meaning to the word, and brought alive its referent. The anxious official appeared in the circular window at infrequent intervals. After an hour he entered with a nurse. He stood behind the stool while the nurse, murmuring as though to a child, prised Mary's fingers from Colin's and walked her to the door.

Mary followed the official along the corridor. As they ascended the stairs, she noticed how the heel of his shoe had worn unevenly. Ordinariness prevailed for an instant, and she had the briefest intimation of the grief that lay in wait. She cleared her throat noisily, and the sound of her own voice drove the thought away.

The young man stepped ahead of her into the brilliant sunshine, and waited. He set down his briefcase, adjusted his starched white shirt cuffs, and courteously, with the faintest of bows, offered to walk her back to the hotel.

Ian McEwan
First Love, Last Rites £1.25

Under Ian McEwan's manipulations, depravity may take on the guise of innocence and butterflies can become sinister. With equal power, he can show a child's life become fouled by the macabre, or distil the awakening sensations of first love, tracing its ritual initiations and infusing them with a luxuriant sensual imagery.

'A brilliant performance, showing an originality astonishing for a writer still in his mid twenties' ANTHONY THWAITE, OBSERVER

In Between the Sheets £1.50

First Love, Last Rites, Ian McEwan's first volume of stories and winner of the 1976 Somerset Maugham Award, was rapturously received as the work of a brilliantly original new writer. Here now is his second collection, as dark, dangerous and funny as the first.

'The most exciting fiction writer in England under thirty' PETER LEWIS, DAILY MAIL

'Exact, tender, funny, voluptuous, disturbing' THE TIMES

The Cement Garden £1.50

'In many ways a shocking book, morbid, full of repellent imagery – and irresistibly readable ... the effect achieved by McEwan's quiet, precise and sensuous touch is that of magic realism' NEW YORK REVIEW OF BOOKS

'A little masterpiece of appalling fascination' DAILY MAIL

'For a first novel, it is a darkly impressive piece of work ... a touch of real fictional genius' THE TIMES

'Just about perfect' SPECTATOR

Picador

☐	The Beckett Trilogy	Samuel Beckett	£2.75p
☐	Making Love: The Picador Book of Erotic Verse	edited by Alan Bold	£1.50p
☐	Willard and His Bowling Trophies	Richard Brautigan	£1.25p
☐	Bury My Heart at Wounded Knee	Dee Brown	£3.75p
☐	The Price Was High, Vol. 1: The Last Uncollected Stories of F. Scott Fitzgerald	edited by Matthew Bruccoli	£2.95p
☐	The Road to Oxiana	Robert Byron	£2.50p
☐	Our Ancestors	Italo Calvino	£3.50p
☐	Auto Da Fé	Elias Canetti	£2.95p
☐	Exotic Pleasures	Peter Carey	£1.50p
☐	In Patagonia	Bruce Chatwin	£2.25p
☐	Sweet Freedom	Anna Coote and Beatrix Campbell	£1.95p
☐	Crown Jewel	Ralph de Boissiere	£2.75p
☐	One Hundred Years of Solitude	Gabriel Garcia Márquez	£2.75p
☐	Nothing, Doting, Blindness	Henry Green	£2.95p
☐	The Obstacle Race	Germaine Greer	£5.95p
☐	Household Tales	Brothers Grimm	£1.50p
☐	Meetings with Remarkable Men	Gurdjieff	£2.75p
☐	Roots	Alex Haley	£3.50p
☐	Growth of the Soil	Knut Hamsun	£2.95p
☐	When the Tree Sings	Stratis Haviaras	£1.95p
☐	Dispatches	Michael Herr	£1.95p
☐	Riddley Walker	Russell Hoban	£1.95p
☐	Stories	Desmond Hogan	£2.50p
☐	Three Trapped Tigers	G. Cabrera Infante	£2.95p
☐	Unreliable Memoirs	Clive James	£1.75p
☐	China Men	Maxine Hong Kingston	£1.50p
☐	The Ghost in the Machine	Arthur Koestler	£2.75p
☐	The Memoirs of a Survivor	Doris Lessing	£1.95p
☐	Albert Camus	Herbert Lottman	£3.95p
☐	The Road to Xanadu	John Livingston Lowes	£1.95p
☐	The Cement Garden	Ian McEwan	£1.50p
☐	The Serial	Cyra McFadden	£1.75p

☐	**McCarthy's List**	Mary Mackey	£1.95p
☐	**Short Lives**	Katinka Matson	£2.50p
☐	**The Snow Leopard**	Peter Matthiessen	£2.50p
☐	**A Short Walk in the Hindu Kush**	Eric Newby	£1.95p
☐	**Wagner Nights**	Ernest Newman	£2.50p
☐	**The Best of Myles**	Flann O'Brien	£2.75p
☐	**Autobiography**	John Cowper Powys	£3.50p
☐	**Hadrian the Seventh**	Fr. Rolfe (Baron Corvo)	£1.25p
☐	**On Broadway**	Damon Runyon	£1.95p
☐	**Midnight's Children**	Salaman Rushdie	£2.95p
☐	**Snowblind**	Robert Sabbag	£1.95p
☐	**The Best of Saki**	Saki	£1.75p
☐	**The Fate of the Earth**	Jonathan Schell	£1.95p
☐	**Sanatorium under the Sign of the Hourglass**	Bruno Schultz	£1.50p
☐	**Miss Silver's Past**	Josef Skvorecky	£2.50p
☐	**Visitants**	Randolph Stow	£2.50p
☐	**Alice Fell**	Emma Tennant	£1.95p
☐	**The Flute-Player**	D. M. Thomas	£2.25p
☐	**The Great Shark Hunt**	Hunter S. Thompson	£3.50p
☐	**The New Tolkien Companion**	J. E. A. Tyler	£2.95p
☐	**Female Friends**	Fay Weldon	£2.50p
☐	**The Outsider**	Colin Wilson	£2.50p
☐	**The Kandy-Kolored Tangerine-Flake Streamline Baby**	Tom Wolfe	£2.25p
☐	**Mars**	Fritz Zorn	£1.95p

All these books are available at your local bookshop or newsagent, or can be ordered direct from the publisher. Indicate the number of copies required and fill in the form below

6

....

Name_____
(Block letters please)

Address_____

_____

Send to Pan Books (CS Department), Cavaye Place, London SW10 9PG
Please enclose remittance to the value of the cover price plus:
35p for the first book plus 15p per copy for each additional book ordered
to a maximum charge of £1.25 to cover postage and packing
Applicable only in the UK

While every effort is made to keep prices low, it is sometimes
necessary to increase prices at short notice. Pan Books reserve
the right to show on covers and charge new retail prices which
may differ from those advertised in the text or elsewhere